Abo

The author and his pa[...]
house, to live in Hertf[...]
Forest. He works for John Lewis, mainly from home, but
still ventures into Central London a couple of days a week.

He's an avid Arsenal fan and enjoys cross country
running, pubs and Caribbean cooking; and of course,
writing. His literary influences include the work of
Ellis Peters, T H White, and the Welsh legends of the
Mabinogion.

His dream is to be writing full time from a luxury cabin in
the bottom of the garden and to see his work make it onto
the big screen.

Dedication

To Den, of course, and to my nephews Charlie and Jez.

E. L. Grant

PRINCE OF THE SOMMERLINGS

BOOK ONE
Kingdom of Elbion

AUSTIN MACAULEY PUBLISHERS™

LONDON • CAMBRIDGE • NEW YORK • SHARJAH

A CIP catalogue record for this title is available from the British Library.

ISBN 9781528998246 (Paperback)
ISBN 9781528998253 (ePub-e-book)

www. austinmacauley. com

First Published 2022
Austin Macauley Publishers Ltd
1 Canada Square
Canary Wharf
London
E14 5AA

Acknowledgements

To Amanda Clark for your beautiful artwork,
and to Kim McSweeney for all your help over the years

Introduction

BEFORE this long tale begins I am sure you are wondering, what is a sommerling?

Well, they are the little creatures of myth and legend, to you and me, they would be from the realm of faery; elves, sprites, pixies and their nemesis, goblin; now living secretly in the shadow of rock, hedgerow and tree; always unseen and always unheard.

Once, before the coming of mortals, they occupied a great sommerling realm called Gilindon; but then as a great evil descended upon their world, as this book will describe, they became scattered and so left Gilindon and descended into a newly found secret world, a place so hidden, so guarded, that the shadow of evil could not follow.

The sommerlings found this new green realm more beguiling than the forbidding lands that they were forced to leave behind. It became their eternal Sommerlands, a place of enchantment and beauty, the land of Fey.

But their greatest fears would always linger in the shadows, a fear of the old evil and the newly arrived mortals, trying to enter their hidden kingdom, for it was foretold that the new settlers of their once great realm Gilindon would one day spell their doom. And so, for a thousand years, their many secret doors remained shut.

This tale entwines two kingdoms, the hidden realm of the sommerlings and the mortal land they left behind, now locked away behind many guarded doors; a kingdom called Elbion (once many, many years ago the land of Britain, but that's another story).

The sommerlings though need not fear Elbion yet, for the mortal island has its own dangers to face, dangers too horrific to imagine, from the old evil that has re-awoken and which is called Morgalene.

Soon, it will be the little kingdom of Elbion that seeks help and in its time of need, can the Prince of the Sommerlings, the very spirit of nature, rescue both mortal and faery lands alike?

The Sommerling Calendar

January	. . . .	Jorbleak
February	. . . .	Fieldstir
March	. . . .	Haregeda
April	. . . .	Budlingar
May	. . . .	Flowerflud
June	. . . .	Glimmering
July	. . . .	Fodil
August	. . . .	Harvengather
September	. . . .	Blackenberry
October	. . . .	Ortumnal
November	. . . .	Nevverend
December	. . . .	Wingloom

Prologue

FIRSTLY, it is to the mortal land of Elbion that we look, a land now free from the faint footfall and cheery laughter of the sommerling; save for a few brave and hardy wanderers.

It is now almost a thousand years since their retreat into the hidden kingdom, yet some still return, passing through the many secret doors, to creep silently amongst the fields and woods, ever curious at the mortal folk now living there. These wandering creatures call it their Galadris, or garden and their hearts are heavy when they have to leave.

They dwell forever between both kingdoms, strangely drawn to both lands, slipping back, under pain of death, through some unguarded door; each sommerling having their reason to risk such a fate.

The mortal year is 1071 and the season was settling into the middle of spring. Yet though there was a new freshness in the air and the lifeless grey limbs of branches now began to show their first colour of white and yellow, the new beginning held little joy for the tall figure who strode purposefully around his cluttered study.

He was a well-proportioned individual, cheery by nature and an extremely respected magician, famed throughout the kingdom as a healer and an expert in all matters concerning mother nature.

Now though, after a falling out with the Grand Wizard five years previously and his subsequent retirement to the countryside, his shoulders were weighed down by the enormity of his new task.

He paused momentarily and looked out of the small round window. Briefly, his mind softened as he gazed westwards to the pretty gardens beyond.

He stroked his short-clipped beard of white and thought of how his long, adventurous life had led to this moment.

Though he had the face of an old man, his eyes still sparkled as brightly as an eager youth. He had seen the passing of many years, most lost now in the mists of his mind. Some years he cherished owing to a particular season that had brought him happy memories, other years were dark, too dark to dwell on.

He reached into a basket and tossed another log upon the fire. The embers danced up and floated into the chimney shaft. He had sat in front of many fires, drunk many wines and had lost his heart to many an enchanting beauty. He had lived amongst mortals for long enough now. Although he cherished their company, he was getting old. He had lived many varied lives, assumed many different names, most names belonging to a distant past. Yet he had kept his great secret intact.

He knew that the current life he had lived for the last eighty years was drawing to a close. Being the spirit of nature was at times so very tiring. Soon it would be time to be reborn, to assume a new mortal name.

For the last thousand or so years, his job had been easy, though his fading memory often obscured the distant past. He had had many mortal names over the years, from Barahar to Mindulin, to Merlin, Herne and Dee and now Nuner.

He had observed the passing seasons, year after year, century after century, fleeting memories now. "My, how the seasons pass so quickly," he said to himself; with a sigh of exasperation. He threw another log upon the fire. Despite being April the air was decidedly chill.

Now the time had come for perhaps his greatest ever task, an errand from Bronia herself, to investigate the strange new rumours. He wondered whether the power within his mask would hold strong after all those years. A once dormant evil had reawakened and maybe the darkest year of all was set to flourish.

Something, he knew not what, had awoken Morgalene the witch. He sighed at the thought and shook his head, aware of what the consequences would be.

Outside, the skeletal arm of a still leafless oak scratched the glass of his study window. He turned to look at the sound and noticed that as dusk was covering her blanket, the first stirrings of an oncoming storm were creeping in from the east. He turned and gazed into the crackling and hissing fire.

Ahead was to be his greatest task of all, to protect the land from Morgalene. He smiled grimly then climbed to his feet. He breathed heavily with the effort and was suddenly surprised at how old he had become.

With his trusty walking stick firmly in his grasp, he left the warmth of the hearth and stepped out from his enchanting thatched cottage, into the gloom of the night. There he stood gazing out across his gardens and the rising, shadowy folds of meadows and fields that surrounded his magical home. He often compared the four seasons to his beloved four wives; whose abiding memories continued to haunt him with sorrow, even after so many years. What were their names?

Ah yes, sweet Nimerlai, she was a sommerling, the fairest one of all, his springtime maid, blue of eye and fair of hair. She so loved her flowers and garden. A tear fell down his cheek.

Then there was his summer bride, enticing and mortal. She too had blue eyes and long braids of light-brown hair. She loved to dance and sing, always laughing under the sun and smiling. Bogeldamead, sweet Bogeldamead. A tear rolled down his other cheek. He could smell their scent now, their perfume was so sweet. He missed them all so much and wondered if any were watching over him.

After summer came his autumn bride, with deep green

eyes and red-gold hair. Faylenseth was her name; a temptress true, with a magical smile. For she was a nymph, a reed maiden. Ah! That was so long ago in his memory. How his heart had been broken. All of his wives beguiled him still. For years, he had locked them in a deep chamber of his mind and now, as the storm gathered, he at last shed tears for them all.

Then last of all was his winter flower, how could he forget. As beautiful and sweet as freshly gathered snowdrops. She was the only light when darkness came, an enticing creature with mortal and sommerling blood and long, raven-black hair. Her smile melted the frosts faster than any fire. She had captured his heart many years before when he had worn a different smile. He sighed heavily and gripped his walking stick ever more tightly. What was her name, he thought, his last true love? Snowfayel, sweet Snowfayel. She had the whitest skin, the reddest lips.

"How I miss you all!" he cried. He then sniffed loudly and wiped another tear away.

So peaceful was his life now, he almost resented this new intrusion. He would miss his garden this summer, for his task would have to begin soon. A sudden chill wind swept down from the dark fields before him and cut through him like a knife. "April's breath is still raw.

I think it is time to put on my green cloak once more," he sighed.

He could feel the walking stick stir at his side. "Well,

dear Eldsmoreth, we have much work to do now before midsummer, a young keeper of the gardens to find and of course beloved Rosewene."

ELBION

1

Eldsmoreth

The Tale Begins

THE moon was yellow, the stars were bright. The long shadow cast by the vast fortress of Grizilder could not yet devour, or destroy, the beautifying soft radiance of their guiding light. It comforted the lean, youthful figure as he darted within that evil realm. He moved with a strange mixture of fear, horror and yet sadness, as he sped along a wide-open passage that ran alongside the battlements. There were many iron-clad doors lining the route, all fixed open and each no doubt leading into some unknown and terrifying place, there were also numerous narrow alleyways feeding off into a dark void, of which there would be no return; these cobweb-draped openings seemed to beckon to him on either side, whispering to him and enticing him to enter. The black alley to his left offered him a chance of escape, its soft voice fluttering the cobwebs as it spoke, while the narrow door to his right promised him many riches, if only he would cross the threshold and enter.

He clutched his true love firmly to his body and could feel her warmth as she pressed into him once more. He knew the spells laid upon her may never be undone and a grim sadness crept over him, a feeling far removed from the elation he had of freeing her from the dungeons. He looked up and felt his long hair move in a sudden warm breeze. He gazed to his left and peered beyond a small open door where only pitch shadow lurked beyond. The stench inside made him flinch.

"Eldsmoreth," came a whispered voice, "come, enter my domain and rest, yes, rest you will."

He stared for a moment, then pulled away and began to run, resisting the hypnotic voice. He moved at a quicker pace, he had to escape this place of nightmare and shadow. The slimy blackened stones beneath his feet had worn the soles of his boots and he could feel the dampness of his own blood mixing with the filth below. Suddenly, he felt a hand pull at his cloak, yet when he turned, there was nobody, nothing, but retreating fingers of shadow; again the moonbeams lit his route and helped keep at bay whatever evil lay in wait for him. He knew that Morgalene and her magic would never let him go, that maybe he was running into a trap. Yet on he sped, along that never-ending bleak passage, past the whispering doors, all gaping open with blackened smiles and the hideous narrow alleyways that sloped down from either side. The passage he followed then began to drop down and turn sharply to the right; he ran past the last open door and the last alley, from each void there came a harsh whisper.

"You will never escape with your beloved," they hissed. "Morgalene will soon be feasting upon your bones!"

The doors that he had fled past then began to creak heavily and with a terrible pounding slammed shut one by one, he was relieved to have resisted the many temptations. "You have given me strength, my love," he said soothingly to the bundle in his arms.

The walls reared up on either side, with small round windows set deep into the rough stone. Had he chosen the right path away from the throne room, there were after all many passageways, many secret doors and many torch-lit hallways; but he had chosen the path north, for that was where he had to escape. He had escaped the inner vaults of the castle, fled along the battlements and now stood in the final courtyard, just before the towering north gates. There was still no movement, no sound. The spells of slumber were heavy and he was pleased with his own magic, but he knew the foul creatures would soon wake. They would smell his blood and come for him with a vengeance. But most of all he dreaded Morgalene, to gaze once more upon her hideous countenance.

He paused, trying hard to catch his breath. He looked up and saw Grizilder`s high-pointed towers, all five of them thrusting like a clawed hand into the putrefying night sky. As he stared in the now fading light, he could see large winged creatures, bat or bird he couldn't tell, circling the high towers at great speed. He could hear their foul cries as they wheeled and dived. These must have been the first to awake. He knew now the hunt was on.

He could feel Rosewene warm under his cloak as she seemed to press nearer to him once again. Maybe the spell of binding could be broken, for the magic was fresh. Her spirit had not died and was yet living within the sword. He gazed down, stroked the blade and whispered to her a spell of enchantment.

Then he turned and ran as fast as his lithe body could muster and from behind, on the ever-encroaching foul wind, he could hear fell voices, the harsh tongue of her servants and then he heard the scream. At first he heard a muttering, one that grew louder and more pronounced. The muttering came to his left, then right, then behind him, as if it were searching for its victim. His ears then pricked up, for the muttering was above his head. The hideous scream that followed rushed down toward him like a vengeful spirit, splitting his ears and clawing at his eyes. It knocked him off his feet and he dropped his beloved and as she fell to the hard stones below, her metal body clattered loudly.

Then the scream ended and Eldsmoreth was on his knees. Morgalene had found him.

At that moment, when all was lost and the only comfort in that grim courtyard was the soft light of the yellowing moon, he heard a gentle voice; the words seemed to rise up and then wash over him like surf on some distant shore.

"Eldsmoreth, my love, my prince," came the words so sweet.

He reached down for the sword and held it tightly once more. He gazed at his beloved with wonder as a soft golden light radiated out and covered his crouching body.

The shimmering sword seemed to ward off the gathering clouds of black mist that had billowed out from the many windows of the castle. The mist had no form and from its swirling, writhing mass, he could hear the evil mutterings once again.

But Rosewene's light held firm and harnessed the youth with strength, waking him from his dull senses. Then her words came again, as a tide returns to the shore. "Eldsmoreth, listen, my power is waning, I cannot protect you for long. I need to sleep. Hold me closer for I can feel your beating heart."

"Oh, my sweet," he sighed heavily. "I have failed you and I have failed Gilindon."

He climbed to his feet and held Rosewene close. Though her warmth was beginning to dim, strength had returned to his body. Tears began to well in his eyes as he knew he was losing his true love again; he now wanted to stay with her to the end and his death which will surely follow, would now be a welcome release.

Rosewene suddenly moved in his grasp and burnt him, she was angered at his thoughts. "I am not dying but sleeping, my dear Eldsmoreth and I want you to escape, to live and to come to me once more."

"I will never leave you," he cried, for he was but a youth.

"I know my sister's magic and I can break her dark charms," she whispered. "Soon her gate will open and an old friend will appear, for I have called him."

Beyond the glimmering tall form of Eldsmoreth, who still clutched the sword to his chest, the dark clouds of mist swirled and writhed like a serpent waiting to strike. Hissed words of venom first issued threats and then tried to beguile him. Suddenly, the sound of many foul horns took to the air and in an instant the mist began to part and then seep away to the many dark pits and recesses of the castle.

Rosewene now shook under his grasp as her final act of magic played out. "I can feel my darkened sister, she is getting closer, we have to fly!"

Suddenly, there came a heavy grinding and the large courtyard gate started to rattle as if an unseen power was trying to break them down and one by one the heavy iron brackets came loose, their thick bolts sang loudly as they whistled through the air; some bolts flew just over Eldsmoreth's stricken form and hit with force some ghouls that were massing on the edge of the courtyard. He could hear their startled cries as the iron swept through them without mercy.

When he looked up, the gates of that gaping monster were wide open and standing on the rocky ground beyond was his old friend. "Merion, it is you," he gasped, though overjoyed his weariness had drained him. The white horse raised his head in recognition and shook his long mane.

"Take me home, my love," said Rosewene, softly. "Take me back to the rose gardens, to where we danced and sang and when all was fair and green."

Just then an arrow flew above his head, then another arrow clattered to the cobbles at his feet. He could hear the hideous roar as Morgalene's host surged forward and came into view; the moonbeams lit up their gnarled and ugly features, their raised axes and their black armour.

More arrows bounced off the shimmering orb of golden light that still bathed and protected Eldsmoreth; an arrow of fire was repulsed and sent flying back into the advancing ghouls, causing panic and more screams of fury.

Eldsmoreth was fast, in one swift movement he turned and ran, there was no match for the youthful elf, he was soon at the towering wooden gates and barely noticed the rows of grimacing skulls that decorated Grizilder's mouth. No sooner than he had leapt upon Merion's back, there came a great rumbling and grinding from behind and then a scream that split the ears.

"My sister is here," gasped Rosewene. "Faster Merion, fly, fly like the wind!" Eldsmoreth pressed his legs tightly to Merion's side and looked back to Grizilder. The hideous castle glowered back at him with malevolence. Even as they sped away over the raised causeway that crossed over the never-ending marsh, he knew they hadn't escaped, that there was still many leagues to cover.

Morgalene's giant black chariot swung into view; Eldsmoreth watched in horror as it seemed Merion`s speed was slowing as though they were being sucked back into the mouth of that monster.

Then he could feel scratches upon his face and he cried out in pain. He clutched at his face and nearly dropped Rosewene, Merion slowed his pace to a canter and he could feel the horse labour and breath heavily. What dark magic was this? Morgalene was pulling them back!

Morgalene stood atop a large moving chariot that was decorated with many skulls, both mortal and faery alike. Her tall frame towered over the two ghoulish servants that were at her side, their spears not even reaching their queen's shoulders. Two large creatures, for in Eldsmoreth's eyes they were not horses, pulled the chariot laboriously as it rumbled from the open gates and down the steep ramp to the wide causeway.

"Stop!" came a harsh voice, so powerful, that it resounded out from the castle and swept across the vast expanse of marsh and reached as far as the brooding, encircling mountains of Undain.

Merion reared up and then cried out as if in great pain, then in a moment of frailty, fell to his knees and so sending Eldsmoreth falling to the blackened earth. Around him swirled the foul-smelling odours of the marsh, their weaving tendrils stroking his limp body and caressing the motionless white form of Merion. Impish specks of light flitted excitedly before his eyes and he could hear voices, not the foul fell language of Morgalene's servants, but these were childlike, with their whispers and giggles. But the moment Eldsmoreth reached out a hand to touch and before one curious light could rest on his upturned hand there came a scream and the lights suddenly extinguished and vanished back down into the dark green mire.

From behind, the tall form of Morgalene moved ever nearer, her chariot being pulled by two monstrous horned beasts was deliberately slow. Saliva fell from her large protruding jaw and she clicked her gnarled and clawed hands. She so needed new bones to feast and fresh blood to bathe in.

"Shall I whip the grimlings?" croaked the taller of the two servants. The other servant, a particularly ugly hob, flinched and almost dropped his spear.

She turned her large head and stooped down until her face was level with the guard. He looked at her in awe and remembered a time when she was wholesome and innocent. Now he shook in fear.

"A meal is best anticipated, there is no need to rush," she resumed her upright position, while her neck clicked in response. The giant chariot rumbled out from Grizilder and moved slowly and with menace toward the stricken elf and horse.

Morgalene smiled to herself, for she could feel her

sister's presence once again. She loathed her but missed her. As for the princeling, well he could be her plaything, oh, what fate would she have in store for him! Then the hideous white horse, so pure, so tasty.

The wheels rumbled on, high above the putrid marsh; yet the odours still floated up, always seeping into the land between the mountains with its scent of the dead. For many years before a great battle had been fought and death still stalked the land. The spirits of the departed had long gone, but some remained, not many and in the form of yellow lights they would often rise up and play, to dance upon their permanent green carpet. As Morgalene and her host moved over their kingdom, their playground, so the spirits became emboldened. The small lights appeared along the route once more, some motionless, just staring at this strange sight, others flitted and danced between the grasses and limpless stalks.

Morgalene glanced to her side and smiled as she breathed in that heady air, so different to the perfumed stench of home. She paid the lights little attention as she neared the doomed rider. There were now a thousand small willo-imps gathered upon the surface. Some had taken on elvish form, though their size was tiny, and to the faery-bank they crawled all the time whispering like excited children. "Yes, a strange site indeed Tom," whispered Dil, his long-standing friend. "The old hag has not left her home in years."

"Did you feel the magic of the boy?" said the first willoimp. "I almost rested upon his hand." The creatures of the mire despised Morgalene, though most feared her. For she had taken their earth-lives years before. Yet, these willo-imps were lucky, or unlucky depending on your view of life; for these were the souls of the bravest and fairest of the fey, still allowed to walk abroad. It was Morgalene who had put them there.

"Quick," shouted Tom, who took on the role of leader, "Let us help get the boy with the sword back upon that fair mount."

There was a rushed urgency as a thousand yellow lights formed into a mass orb and briefly hovered over the stagnant marsh air and descended at speed to the sleeping Merion. They raised the confused horse and with an ease of strength and with the humming of a thousand excited voices lifted Eldsmoreth into a sitting position. They handled Rosewene with care and love, for they could feel an enchantment from the sword, but were confused. It was a scent they had smelt before; like smelling the first bluebell of spring after an eternal winter.

"Careful now," whispered Dil as he oversaw the waking of the boy. "Take her," he urged, wrapping the youth's fingers around the hilt of Rosewene.

Eldsmoreth stirred, Merion was alert once again and Roswene emitted a soft golden glow. The willo-imps backed away in a single mass and then when their work was done, split into a thousand darting lights.

The first of Morgalene`s ghouls were upon the lights in

a rage, waving their axes in vain as they cursed in anger. Some carried nets that they swung in the night air, some imps were taken, shrieking in terror as they landed in the traps.

Morgalene jumped from the chariot in a fury, her servants scurried to get out of her way, dismayed at her power and her height. She held now a gleaming knife in her right hand and strode toward Merion and Eldsmoreth. Her appearance was hideous to behold as her pointed iron boots crunched upon the ground below and her seven-foot frame towered over the smaller hobs that had formed her guard. She kicked one unfortunate hob who was in her way, down the causeway bank and into the marsh below, his cry of help went unnoticed as he succumbed to the embrace of that clinging, green deathbed.

"Sister, come to me," she screamed. She crushed one imp upon her shoulder, one that had the misfortune to land there. "I want his blood; I want his bones and I want that horse's head!" A collection of willo-imps, led by Tom, gathered behind Merion and pushed with a force that jolted both rider and horse from their drowsiness and swiftly back into the terror of their predicament.

"Flee!" shouted the imps as Morgalene reached out with her clawed hand, her long nails protracting in and out. Eldsmoreth could feel her foul breath on his neck and shuddered as he felt a long nail scrape down his back and begin to rip his tunic. The imps suddenly exploded into a haze of flitting lights as Morgalene's terrible shadow loomed over Merion.

Up reared the white horse and off he sped, away from the grasp of the witch and away from the castle Grizilder. Merion was the fastest horse in Gilindon, a prized gelding who now had urgent business. Neither looked behind, but both could hear the screams of Morgalene mixed with the exciting chatterings of the willow-imps, who in turn began luring many hobs down into the green mire, where they were led many years before.

Eldsmoreth's journey north was like a dream, his body and mind, for one so young, clung to a sense of purpose, to take his beloved back to her rose gardens and her favourite magnolia tree. Beyond the causeway the track bore them over the last furlongs of the marshes. There were scattered lights that would rise to greet them then dive back down again, nervous as to the strange sight before them.

Night passed into day as they left the marshes and pressed on at relentless speed through a narrow ravine, which was dark and ominous, as the last mountains of Undain pressed in on either side. Rocks would drop from a great height and fall about them, crashing and rolling amongst the thin bushes of scrub. As they journeyed on, Eldsmoreth's mind drifted into a deep dream as Rosewene pressed into his chest. Her power had resurged, as she knew she would be back in the gardens of Liminulin once again and in her heart, she felt joy. She warmed her beloved as she felt his breath and tremble in his sleep.

Day turned into night and still, Merion raced on. Eldsmoreth stirred under that starry night sky, yet the crescent shape moon, now a silvery hue, peeped out from behind some black cloud. In the distance to their left was a brooding shadow of trees, it was the great forest of Lineer. Though it was over a mile away they could hear strange and menacing sounds coming from within its twisted and ancient eaves.

The following morning they rested by a stream, the soft music of its chattering brought both elf and horse a sense of calm and happiness. In the deeper reeds just beyond where the long grass grew by the bank, a maiden watched and breathed heavily. She had not seen such a comely youth before. But as he sat away from the reeds and appeared to be sleeping, her enchantment could not work on him. She looked at her reflection and saw her beauty smiling back. She was a creature of the tumbling beck and the earth was not for her. She sighed deeply and disappeared with a splash back under the surface. Eldsmoreth heard a sound, looked up and gazed over to the rustling reeds.

Later in the afternoon they crossed a deep river where many stones were piled and pressed relentlessly on. Their spirits were lifted as they heard birdsong once again and Eldsmoreth began to sing.

Merion waved his ears and the elf laughed, "Sorry, my

dear friend, but I have been told my voice is the sound of many harps." Merion showed his teeth and Eldsmoreth's laughter came as the sun finally appeared and the sky was blue once more.

As the night came, they rested once more, but as they camped amongst a circle of silver birch, Merion began to stir. His ears pricked up and he straightened his rear leg. He turned to the south and sniffed the air. Eldsmoreth came to his side and ran his long fingers through his mane. "What do you hear, old friend?" he paused. "All I can hear is a soft wind through the linden leaves."

In the morning Merion continued at a pace. Later in the day they found the open land narrowing between a large forest of bright green, in the west and to their right, in the east, was a comely collection of rounded hills. Some of the hills were mere mounds compared to the peaks of Undain, yet there was something appealing in their look. The lands had been rich once, before the darkness came.

Skylarks could be heard as they passed swiftly into more fertile lands. The small brown birds would dart up from their nesting ground, from deep within the long stems and sing their joyous song from high above. The road was well made, level and layered with chalk. The straight route was lined with walls of uneven grey stone, out of which small ferns and wildflowers sprouted from the many gaps. Eldsmoreth was sure he saw swift darting movements coming from the other side and the sound of excited chatterings and chuckles.

Beyond the wall, where the long grass was untended, were neat rows of trees, some apple and some cherry. Fruit hung as ornaments from their ancient, gnarled arms and many were scattered amongst the thick tussocks of grass and scented cow-parsley. The air was rich with fragrance and the busy humming of bees, as a gentle wind from the west swayed the many flowers that grew before the wall. This part of Gilindon was known as the Alba-Gal, which means white stars; for in the Spring, thousands of orchards would suddenly, as one, unveil their white, sweet-scented gowns.

That night they camped before the banks of the Celadin, a wide and swift-running river that flowed from the Arahundel hills in the west, dividing the land in two and eventually flowing out into the eastern seas. Eldsmoreth lit a fire amongst a grove of holly bushes, for though it was summer, the air was chill and a cooling breeze came up from the south.

From above the crackling of the small fire, Eldsmoreth's sharp ears picked up a distant sound. Merion also stirred and shook his long mane. They were far from Grizilder, yet something did not feel right, he was sure he could hear the shrill sound of a horn carried to him on the wind.

He stroked Rosewene tenderly, yet she was cold to touch. His heart sank. There were still many leagues until he could reach the gardens of Liminulin and so break the spell of enduring sleep. Despite his growing fears and doubts, Eldsmoreth succumbed to a deep slumber and when he awoke the fire had died and he could see Merion alert and looking beyond the ancient holly bushes to the road south from where they had come.

Suddenly, Merion turned and nudged his head into the youth. Eldsmoreth knew they had to press on. "I fear Morgalene has tracked us north, my friend," whispered the elf. "We can both feel it in our bones."

Merion shook his mane and motioned Eldsmoreth to climb upon his back.

Though their mood was low and a creeping sense of dread descended over them like a dark cloud, the weather was kind. A full sun emerged from behind the last tailcoat of cloud and did not depart until it set slowly in the west. The white road enhanced the brightness of the day and high above the larks returned, playing their excited tunes to their welcoming ears. By the afternoon they had journeyed deep into the land called Almarion, orchards grew as far as the eye could see, not just the white blossom of apple but the radiant pink of cherry and the bright yellow of pear. Eldsmoreth could see the abandoned small holdings of fruit picker huts with their pointed roofs and broken leaded windows. The sight of desolation, even in such a beautiful setting, filled him with sorrow.

The drystone walls that lined their route soon gave way to lush thick hedgerows that blocked their view as the green wall connected one small copse of oaks with another. Though the land was free of elf-hand, the birds and wildlife still flourished. Eldsmoreth sighed with a heavy heart, as he thought of ways to break Rosewene's spell of slumber. He knew that such magic still enshrined the walls of the rose garden and that the very soil was imbued with enchantment. He knew what had to be done.

The journey continued; Rosewene still lay cold to touch and Merion was silent, save for the rhythmic breathing of his lean body. To his right, Eldsmoreth could see another wide meandering river, where its water shone in a silvery light as the sun danced upon the surface. Merion knew where he was heading and he shook his mane toward the river and snorted loudly.

They left the road and plunged between a gap in the ancient hedgerow; spindly arms of hawthorn pulled at Eldsmoreth's already ragged tunic and his long hair, already matted, was now covered in small white flowers. The elf prince marvelled at Merion's endurance, as he galloped toward the broad river. Such was his speed, he almost thought the gelding would sprout wings and fly across.

Eldsmoreth patted his flank and the horse slowed to a canter, his breathing was hard, yet the legs were sturdy and soon Merion halted and bent to eat the lush grass. His reward after a long, hard journey.

Eldsmoreth sat upright and gazed over to a sight that was once familiar and he knew that the enchanted gardens were at most fifteen leagues away.

The standing stones of Igon loomed tall above the river

which bore the same name; they were ever watchful sentinels that were made by hands unknown. Their bluestone cloaks had endured the lonely passing of time and witnessed the endless cycles of seasons. He gazed in awe at a sight he had not seen for many years. "Glad to see such old friends have not changed, Merion."

Before the setting of the sun, when the light was pleasing and mellow, Eldsmoreth laid down to rest upon the lush meadow with Rosewene laying at his side. He sat atop a flower-strewn bank that eventually rolled down to the lapping of the water's edge. Here, tall reeds swayed in the soft late afternoon breeze, accompanied by the sound of waterfowl venturing back to the safety of their homes before the coming of night.

He was so weary since his escape from Grizilder that the pang of hunger, of which berries from the hedgerow and water from the stream were his only banquet, could not stop him slipping into a deep untroubled sleep under a vast blanket of a billion glittering stars.

The following morning, Eldsmoreth awoke in a panic and started to cough. During the night a mist had risen from the river and now swathed the banks in a thick fog; its clammy fingers wrapping around the bulrushes and burdock and creeping up the banks to higher ground.

He could make out the distant form of Merion as he grazed contentedly upon the long grass and at that moment he began to shiver. He then looked back toward the river and was confused. The mist had not crept up from the Igon but was creeping toward it. The mist was coming from the meadows behind.

He leapt to his feet with Rosewene firmly back in his grasp and climbed the bank in a panic. He could see the small yellow flowers that had displayed their beauty only the evening before, had now wilted and died. His ears pricked up. "She is here!" cried Eldsmoreth, though his words were muffled in the thickening fog. "Her evil is poisoning the land." Merion looked up and noticed the mist for the first time, then he could see the slender youth running toward him. Merion sniffed the air and then stamped his hooves. Seeing Eldsmoreth's terror and sensing an unseen danger, he quickly knelt on his front knees, letting the youth leap with ease upon his back.

Eldsmoreth had been careless, he thought Morgalene would be trapped by her magic within the ring of Undain, but he was wrong. She wanted her sister back to hang in chains above her throne of skulls and what of him and dear Merion. The thick, yellow fog closed in around them as Merion at first turned in a circle, unsure of where to go. "To the river, dear friend," urged the elf. "We cannot go back, for I can smell her foul odours."

Then from out of the swirling mists, which now took the form of dragons heads with snapping jaws, came the small, ugly hobs. These were Morgalene's trackers. They burst into view, cackling and screaming with malice, for they had found the slumberers, the flower sniffers. In their rough hands they wielded small daggers and from their open mouths fell gleeful drops of saliva.

A loud cacophony of trumpets sounded and the clash of symbols. The hunt was on and nearer rolled the heavy grinding of the Witch's chariot. Then there came that hideous voice as it scraped and penetrated the thick blanket of swirling mist, "Where are you elf-boy and where have you hidden my sister?"

Merion reared high and his front hooves kicked an unfortunate hob in the face, sending its scrawny form rolling down the bank and into the reedbeds. A dagger grazed Merion's rear and the pain jolted the horse down toward the river, Eldsmoreth clung to the mane while securing Rosewene through his belt. The terrified horse pushed into the reedbeds and felt the sharp touch of cold water wash over his wound. From within the murky depths the hob that had landed toothless after being kicked, thrust upward a clawed hand and gripped Eldsmoreth's right leg. He pulled his leg free and kicked the hob with force back down into his watery bed.

Morgalene rose high in her chariot, towering above all who had gathered around her form. She raised her arms and cursed aloud. The swirling mists vanished back from the river, on up the bank, retreating and moving toward the caravan of ghouls that had gathered in their foul ranks. As the mist touched the ground, so all the flowers and plants succumbed.

Then Morgalene screamed, the sound causing the

reeds to bend and the water to move. She raised her gnarled walking staff in her right hand and pointed it toward the fleeing youth, "This will be your bed one day, this will be your eternal home."

The gathered ranks of hobs and some of the larger goblin servants looked up in fear and trepidation as the power of their queen was unleashed. They saw the diminishing mist spiral in a depleted dance and then with a final movement rush at speed back toward the black chariot and back into the wide-open cavern of Morgalene's mouth.

Merion could feel the ground below vanish and soon he was treading water, again they could hear the sound of arrows hitting the water all around them, but they were unscathed.

Then the arrows stopped and the sound of the harsh goblin music, coupled with the screeching and cackling, had faded. Eldsmoreth looked back while clinging upon Merion's wet mane. The strange mist had gone and he could see the tall figure of Morgalene standing upon her chariot while at her side were amassed an army of ghouls. He could feel the witch's eyes upon him, burning into his back; yet her magic could not touch him as he waited for her claws to sink into his flesh, or for a giant wave to surge toward them and so drown them. But nothing. Just the tall figure of Morgalene, now standing silent, just pointing the tip of a long walking staff toward his fleeing form.

All was strangely still and silent, just the lapping of Igon's waters as they scrambled at last to the opposite bank and paused for breath under the watchful gaze of the stone sentinels. Here the rare golden flowers of Almarion were scattered over the lush meadows as far as the eye could see. But back beyond the deep water, back south, all was dying and withering. Gilindon would soon be gone forever.

They passed under the watchful shadow of the mighty bluestones and hurried north. Neither wanted to pause for sleep or to light a fire and rest. As the day drew to a close and the sun started to fade into the west, they crossed over a wide stream that still had intact a beautiful white wooden bridge, whose many lanterns swung in the warm night breeze. The last clouds of the night hurried overhead and there was a strong wind blowing in from the south. To their right, they could see the last shadowy outline of some hills that filed away into the south and west, so a full moon lit their way across a land of over-grown hedgerows, dark clusters of trees and the many ordered ranks of solemn orchards.

Eldsmoreth knew the land had been abandoned, even this far north. There were still the tiny flapping and scur-ryings of the little folk, who now sought refuge behind the stone walls, or made homes in the many large boughs of oak. Even the impenetrable hedgerows were home to animal, or imp. They could still hear their merry chatter-ings joining the chorus of blackbird and robin as they passed by. Soon they too would be gone for he had heard of the Land of Fey.

The night soon came and on Merion pressed, though his pace had slowed. Eldsmoreth had offered to walk at his side for a while to ease his burden, but the gelding nudged his head for him to remain. The turf was springy and lush as they followed the line of an ancient hedgerow that ran directly north. They both knew there was a well-made elf-road over to the west, but for good reason they felt safer making their own route.

It was bright dawn when they, at last, came to a small stream that flowed out from a dense thicket of trees, its passage masked by rows of curling ferns.

Merion's ears pricked up at the inviting sound of water, he slowed his pace and then halted. Eldsmoreth climbed from his back and slid Rosewene free. The soft sound of the water soothed his nerves and rekindled many happy memories.

For it was at a spot such as this that he had danced with Rosewene one spring evening. While Merion bent down to drink, Eldsmoreth was thinking back to happier times, to a glade of willow trees by the banks of the Maluin. He closed his eyes and breathed deeply.

Suddenly, Rosewene began to warm and then a soft glow began to radiate as she lay upon the grass by the chattering stream. Eldsmoreth's heart leapt as he saw the life return and he gazed down with tears. "You remember the dance, the sound of the flute and harp!!"

She spoke, but her answer came in such a whisper that he couldn't understand. He held her once more and vowed to break the spell.

They rested longer than planned, for both had fallen into a deep slumber and only awoke when the skies darkened and it began to rain. Eldsmoreth knew that was an omen, he slid Rosewene back into his belt and climbed swiftly upon Merion for the final journey to the rose gardens.

The dark clouds, which had turned into inky blue, were left behind as they sped north. Eldsmoreth kept looking over his shoulder as they neared the gates of Liminulin. The clouds, which were now massing in the south, took on a formidable sight both expanding and billowing as if it were a monster crawling toward them. When he turned a final time, he was sure he saw a malevolent face form and then in an instant vanish.

Merion turned to the west and soon they noticed in the distance the long row of rowan trees that lined the ancient elf road, their berries blazing in a deep red. At last, he could see in the distance the long wall of golden stone that surrounded the fair town of Liminulin. It was a dwelling place of enchantment and magic whose spring waters and music would heal the weary and sick. The town was surrounded by a low stone wall and sat upon the banks of the fast-flowing, Maluin. Once, before the rumour of darkness grew, it was not only a merry and prosperous place but also beguiling and beautiful, famed for the many gardens and orchards that seemed to flower and bear fruit well into the winter.

It was also the home of the princess Rosewene, who, unbeknown to many, had her own secret rose gardens set within her own high wall. Eldsmoreth, who as a young boy had discovered her secret glade and had unknowingly, lifted the magic veil that shrouded her haven of rose and sweetpea.

As they approached the town he could see the gates had been forced apart and the surrounding fields now covered in teasel, thistle and weeds, had grown up to the fading stone walls. Thick tendrils of dark green ivy also covered the outer walls and had crawled, in time, over the ramparts and had started to peep in at the empty windows of the corner towers.

Merion sped through the gates, causing a startled chatter from a large host of sparrows that were foraging for seeds.

Liminulin was abandoned. Ivy not only covered the outer walls and turrets but had crept over every house, through every open window; it wrapped around the sign on the inn, covered the broad drinking troughs, strangled the dovecotes and forced open the lids of ale barrels.

Birds watched their slow progress, as did the small animals, the red squirrels, the inquisitive field hare and the homeless cat. With a heavy heart, Eldsmoreth guided Merion along a narrow lane that led to the river. At the end, set against a high brick wall, the small guard tower with its pointed roof, stood forlorn and cloaked in green. The guards had long gone and to the right, the heavy wooden gate that led to the gardens had been broken.

Eldsmoreth dismounted and peered through the hanging gate into the garden beyond. The curved brick archway was strangely free of ivy, yet instead there grew a protective barrier of thorns, its razor-sharp arms constantly coiled and moved. Some of the sharpened tentacles broke free and investigated the new visitors. Eldsmoreth stood perfectly still as their deadly tendrils stroked his face as delicately as a feather. He gasped in fear as the giant thorns were but inches from his face. Then in an instant, the tendrils pulled back, some whipping through the air, others slithering across the floor. In one swift movement, the arms then began to unravel and soon the large green beast split into two, leaving a gap just wide enough for him to enter through.

Eldsmoreth took Rosewene into his arms and kissed her cold body. The thorns began to coil once more, scraping against the walls either side and then moving out curiously toward him again. He took his beloved and walked through the arch and into the rose garden.

The large garden, though overgrown, was as enchanting as ever. The encircling wall of thin red brick was now hidden by tall columns of rose bushes; their thickened stems had, over time, intertwined and merged into a myriad of jostling petals of purples, reds, whites and yellows.

Before the outer ranks of roses there grew towering hollyhocks of pink whose welcoming umbels were still attracting large bumblebees. The ground where he had first seen Rosewene dance was now rooted with many poppies and long trailing bushes of a white star.

He could feel eyes upon him as he made his way to the south wall and the large brooding limbs of the magnolia tree. He looked up in awe, for the tree had grown since his last visit. Its long sloping arms almost reached the ground, which was covered in a thick bed of fallen white petals, which now browned at the edges.

As Eldsmoreth walked once more in the secret garden, his presence stirred interest from all the small creatures that still dwelt in that green realm. Insects stopped flitting in the warm air, bumblebees forgot about their nectar and the many small birds, the robin and the wren, stopped foraging and came to gaze upon this strange sight.

Eldsmoreth knelt before the magnolia and for a brief moment, all was still. The ancient tree then began to sway as though a sudden breeze had swept through its branches. More white petals fell to the ground falling upon Eldsmoreth's ragged cloak and the form of Rosewene. The elf whispered a charm and then began to dig, at first he used his hands and then he searched for a stick which he then used to break up the rich soil.

The animals looked on in awe for they knew that magic had returned to the gardens. Some of the older birds could sense the presence of their dancing princess but were confused upon seeing just a tall youth and a long pale sword.

Eldsmoreth toiled for many hours, for he had heard her words in his head urging him to return to the garden and the magnolia tree and to bury her deep in the sacred soil. She would be safe there until he could return one day, maybe a year from now, giving her time for the magic of the soil to restore her form.

A robin dropped to his side as he worked, looking at the tempting worms but resisted. Bees began to circle his head and insects rested upon the branches. They could all feel the power of Rosewene. Her blade glinted but Eldsmoreth failed to notice, so gripped was he in his task.

Afternoon turned to evening and he could hear Merion stamping his hooves loudly beyond the garden walls. Eldsmoreth had dug a hole waist height. He gathered a bouquet and wrapped them tenderly around her form. He climbed with her into the deep trench and laid her down with care. Now his task was done he had not the heart to leave his beloved.

She was dressed in a woven blanket of wildflowers as though she were awaiting her wedding in the forest. But this would be no happy occasion.

Eldsmoreth climbed out and began to cover her form with soil. This was no grave he thought, but a bed. Tears filled his eyes as he covered the disturbed patch of soil and he spoke to the tree to protect her while he was gone. To his surprise, the Magnolia spoke to him, in a rich and powerful voice.

"My roots, dear fellow, shall grow around her form like a bower and I shall protect her. She shall sleep safely in my soil. Fear not, for she is dreaming already. She shall wait for you." Eldsmoreth bowed before the mighty magnolia and turned swiftly from the garden. He would return but that would be many, many years later.

2

Trifan Foxley

IT was now the fair month of May and the long harsh winter that had laid siege to the little kingdom of Elbion well into April was but a distant memory, as the once shy spring buds exploded early with vigour and colour across the land, thickening hedgerows and the vast acres of apple-trees that filled the island's many orchards.

But it is to a northern shire, a rich green county, that our attention is drawn and to its pleasant, bustling market town called Oakendale, nestling within a patchwork of green fields and meadows.

It was now early evening, just past seven o'clock and the day's strong sun had descended into the western horizon sending up a fantastical glow of gold and red.

Most of the townsfolk had retired indoors, either to enjoy a large seasonal supper or to visit one of the many welcoming ale-houses.

Even the town's wildfowl had taken their last flight of the evening and had settled down by the broad banks of the River Freshbright, seeking refuge in the numerous reed-beds, or sheltering under a protective feathered wing. The only sound, apart from the music of merrymaking from the nearby Unicorn Inn, came from the old rose gardens, a large yet secretive and forgotten green sanctuary, set within an ancient curved wall of brick.

The gardens fanned out from the foot of Oakendale Castle and its single high turret of yellowing stone.

The noise which now echoed faintly around the walls belonged to a gardener, a boy to be precise, one slightly scruffy in appearance, from his unwashed curly fair hair to his dirt-smeared tunic of dark green. The boy was toiling purposefully away, late, in his appointed task of weeding and planting. The sound was the loud chink of metal upon stone and rock as his trowel dug deep into the fertile flowerbeds.

The boy's name was Trifan, Trifan Foxley, a tall, gangly sixteen-year-old who was orphaned fourteen years earlier after his parents, who were travelling through the town on business from Weffolk, were killed in a lightning storm. It was the church who found him sanctuary, housing and schooling him within the Abbey walls. Trifan, who was now an assistant gardener at the Royal Rose-Gardens, brushed aside his long strands of fair hair from his eyes and wiped the beaded sweat from his brow. He looked down upon the results of the day's toil, of the raking, pruning and planting that had occupied him for hour upon weary hour.

He gazed with a tired pleasure at the tangled mass of

creeping-vine, nettles and dandelion-heads that lay scattered around the borders of the beds. The arduous task to which he had been so cruelly appointed by the head gardener Grimridge early that morning had at last been completed, leaving him little time to go down to the inn or wander to the church meadow and watch the many travellers setting up their stalls for the forthcoming Rose Fayre. But as his weary limbs suggested, he would do neither but go home to bed. Besides, it was early evening and the day's strong sun was at last beginning to disappear behind the single, high turret of Oakendale Castle. He decided he would return early the following morning to finish planting but for the time being, he had other ideas.

Quickly, he loaded his tools into the wheelbarrow and trundled off towards the potting shed that was situated at the northern end of the gardens, nestling under the protective arms of an old, gnarled oak. He cursed Grimridge and the fast-dwindling sun as he went on his way.

It had been an unusually warm spring that particular year in Oakendale and indeed much of Elbion, so much so that even the old folk couldn't remember one so sticky and uncomfortable. There hadn't even been the respite of cool wind to relieve the suffering. He stopped to rest, wiping his brow free of sweat and glanced at the display of roses, now planted neatly in line, their buds peeping through as if awakening from a deep sleep. He smiled with contentment, his long weary day of toil over.

"This really is my kingdom now," he said aloud. He

knew nobody would hear him. The other gardeners had already left for home and they were both half-deaf anyway.

"Every leaf, every bud, every opening flower, even the insects and birds do my bidding!" His clear voice echoed off the high surrounding wall. Nobody challenged his cry, the insects carried on busying themselves, birds just perched and stared and the flower heads kept up their silent, steady gaze. He wondered if the day's sun had sent him into some kind of madness. Was he really losing his mind? His head was full of such strange thoughts, thoughts that for the last month or so had started to creep into his mind. He couldn't quite put his finger on it but it felt as if the garden was watching him; watching as he toiled silently, almost reading his thoughts.

Sometimes he would turn swiftly, only to find the tall ranks of plants looming in their beds behind him and the relentless sun glimmering down.

He didn't like to admit it and he certainly wouldn't mention it to his friends, but he had started talking to the plants. At first, he would whisper words to soothe and encourage but recently he had been talking openly and loudly to them.

It would all have to stop. It was only a garden, enchanting at times admittedly, but only a garden all the same. Just then his ears pricked up, somewhere far off he could hear a cry, startled and full of panic. He turned and wondered where it had come from. Then he heard the cry again. He squinted into the setting sun but could only make out pockets of trees and the high curve of the old west wall. Beyond that, he could see the raised tops of trees from the Queen's Wood. He glanced away from the still simmering sun and rubbed his eyes. Whatever the cry was it came from beyond the walls of his kingdom.

He was surprised that anybody was out. It had been such a hot day that all of Oakendale had retreated inside. Come to think of it, he was probably the only fool out under the sun, even the animals in the fields and meadows had wandered back into their stables, or under the shade of a tree. "Such a strange year," he sighed again. "It's almost as if something peculiar is about to happen."

In fact, it had been a strange year all around for the inhabitants of Elbion, especially for those in the more remote parts of the south and west.

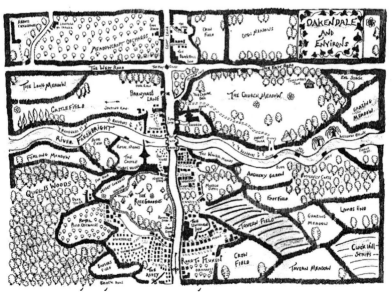

He wiped his brow once more and a new thought entered his weary mind. "That's settled then, I think I'll visit the inn tonight, have a few pints, listen to a gripping tale and then back home to bed." He was pleased he had, at last, made his mind up. Trifan could almost taste the cool ale on his lips as the prospect of sitting in the scented garden of the Unicorn Inn appealed even more. Besides, old Tapwine, the landlord, still owed him, after he had swept his stables.

After much groaning, he at last reached the large potting shed and dropped the wheelbarrow to the grass. His arms ached, as did his back. He thought how the aged Grimridge walked with a permanent stoop and how his joints would often lock. This would explain the old man's vindictive streak and sharp tongue.

"Can't be a gardener all your life," he said loudly, opening the door of the potting shed. "They already call me son of Grimridge." It creaked in its usual welcome, revealing a dark world of flowerpots cobwebs and the damp odour of soil. He wheeled the barrow to the back of the shed and gazed around, appreciating the enchanting qualities of his favourite hideaway.

Whenever he wanted to be alone, he would retreat into the shed, light a lantern or two and sit down to think about his life. He would travel back to the ordered and disciplined life of his school days at Oakendale Abbey, smiling wryly as he remembered smoking pipes at the back of the Unicorn Inn or sneaking over the walls at night to scrump for cherries and apples in the Royal Orchards with his gang of cloistered urchins.

Sometimes, he would try to think about his mother and father but hard as he tried, he couldn't picture their faces, their features would always elude him. A grim sadness crept into his heart, cold fingers of melancholy that wrapped around him blocking out any light. He looked over at the round leaded window and saw the softening sun filtering through the shadows of the old gnarled oak. "Time to leave the shadows I think," he sighed. Suddenly, he heard the familiar cry again but this time, it came from the garden. Trifan wiped the dirt from his hands upon his green tunic and left the dark confines of the shed. He walked out into the sweet-smelling garden and looked around. It was completely empty.

He wondered if somebody was playing a prank. Perhaps it was his imagination, after all he was tired after a long day toiling under the sun, or perhaps it was his friend Edwyn Bracey, who was always playing cruel jokes upon the unsuspecting. Hadn't Edwyn impersonated Grimridge once and tricked him into digging up the Abbot's fruit trees?

"Stop fooling around, Bracey, where are you hiding?" he cried, "I know it's you."

"I'm up here!" replied a much louder voice. "Watch out – I'm going to crash-land!"

Trifan gazed up at the darkening skies and to his horror saw a large, rounded sphere of many colours, like some fat magical beast, descending at speed towards the gardens. Hanging underneath it and suspended from many ropes, appeared to be a large fisherman's basket containing a rather willowy, wizened-looking man wearing a tall wide-brimmed pointed hat and carrying a long-gnarled walking stick.

Trifan ran under one of the trees for cover and watched in stunned silence as the creation dropped from the heavens and crash-landed in the branches of the apple trees lining the wall of the garden.

Then with a loud thud, the large basket containing the strange man dropped upon and flattened the newly planted rose-beds below. For the moment, Trifan feared the worst and cowered behind the trunk of a tree watching with a mixture of horror and intrigue as the man climbed out of the basket and began brushing himself down.

His appearance lived up to Trifan's worst fears. He stood at well over six feet in height and wore a long cloak of dark green that brushed the ground with its heavy material. His hair was as white as the driven snow, as was his clipped beard and bushy eyebrows. Surely this wasn't the dragon of darkness that had terrorised so many dreams?

At last, the old man spoke, although his accent was strange.

"Quite a landing don't you think, eh? I was aiming for

the church meadow, don't you know. Talk about poor control!"

Trifan peered nervously around the trunk of the tree, whereupon his eyes connected with the old man's.

"You don't have to be afraid, my good soul," he continued, "I'm not going to eat you!"

"Who are you?" asked Trifan still feeling apprehensive.

"I am you might say a travelling magician, my young fair-haired friend. You can call me Tumlinfay. Mr Tumlinfay. And this…," he said pointing to the wreckage behind, "Was an invention of mine, the incredible flying dragon. Alas broken, a little like your garden for which I apologise."

"It's not my garden," replied Trifan cautiously, "I wish it was. I am just the keeper here, the assistant gardener."

Suddenly, the old man took off his hat and appeared to gaze with wonder around the garden while muttering a rhyme under his breath.

"Amid roses of red and leaf of green, there dwells the keeper young and keen."

He returned his gaze to Trifan once more and smiled his warm smile.

"You are indeed a lucky young man to find yourself working in such pleasant surroundings. Ah! There's something magical about gardens, a haven of beauty, secrets, colour and dreams."

"If you don't mind me asking," said Trifan, curious

about the old man and still trying to work out what he had muttered. "Did you really drop down from the sky?"

Tumlinfay laughed out loud as his eyes glinted brightly in the deepening gloom.

"My dear sir, it may have appeared like dropping to you but I have floated from the Shire of Fluxen to be here today. My dragon can take me anywhere. It is a simple contraption of hot air, a basket, a few ropes and some dyed canvas."

Trifan cast an anxious glance at the mass of canvas and ropes and the giant basket that had so flattened his most prized rose bed by the wall. Grimridge is never going to believe this, he thought.

"You have no need to worry, young man," replied Tumlinfay almost reading his mind. "When I have repaired my invention, I shall even take you for a ride in it but for the time being would you be so kind as to help me salvage my dragon as I am late for a very important date."

Trifan duly obliged and assisted the old man in untangling the rope and canvas from the apple tree and rose bushes.

After packing the remainder of his flying machine and baggage into the basket, Tumlinfay turned to Trifan, "If you could look after this for me I'll be much indebted."

Trifan found himself accepting the strange man's request without hesitation. "I suppose I could store it behind the potting shed for a few days."

"Right then I'll be off now," said Tumlinfay, picking up his long-gnarled walking stick with a sense of urgency.

"Where are you going? If you don't mind me asking," enquired Trifan.

"To the Rose Fayre my good man. I have a tent and stall waiting for me. I shall be there over the next three days. If you pop over, I'll show you a few tricks for free!"

Then the strange man turned on his heel, waved a fare-well and headed in the direction of the northern gates singing a cheery song as he went:

"Come with me to Oakendale Fayre,
Where the sweet smells of summer fill the air,
As hand in hand, we shall go,
Down to the meadow to see the show."

When the magician reached the ivy-clad archway of the northern gate, he called out loudly, "I almost forgot young man, what is your name?"

"Trifan!" replied the boy swiftly, "Trifan Foxley."

The old man returned a warm smile and then vanished from view.

Later on that evening in his room in the castle tower, Trifan found himself falling asleep almost as soon as his head rested upon his pillow. At first, he dreamt only of pleasurable things, like the rose garden in summer, butterflies dancing upon the wind and swans sailing upon the River Freshbright.

Then he saw the old man beckoning to him and the

dream began to sour. Snow began to fall all around him covering the garden with its thick whiteness and destroying the colour before his eyes. Then the shadows began to grow, darkness the like of which he had never seen before, covering not only the garden and Oakendale but also his very heart. It was almost as if the spring and summer were lost forever as all-around lay suffocating and dying. Then the strange Mr Tumlinfay came into view, he appeared to be holding a sturdy bough of yew, not the crooked walking stick and upon his lips, a smile began to form. Then the strange dream faded into darkness and stillness.

3

The Tomb of Morgalene

THAT same year and also in spring (though the landscape suggested winter), deep in the uninhabited wasteland called Mortenden, four magicians, three of mortal blood and wizened in appearance, while the fourth, who was shorter and of sommerling blood, crept their way through the dark vaults and suffocating passageways of a grim castle.

The castle was once, many, many years before, the lair of a demoness, called Morgalene.

It was now nothing more than a tomb, an abandoned fortress hidden within a treacherous circle of enchanted mountains.

The group had, after five years of fruitless searching, come within touching distance of the ultimate prize.

The sommerling's name was Grib, a particularly loathsome individual of unusually large size. The sommerling turned to face the three mortals. He held aloft a flickering firebrand, which lit up his thin face and enormous pointed nose.

"Welcome to Grizilder, the lair of our most terrible queen, Madame Morgalene. Can you not smell her greatness?"

His words were harsh and as ugly as his appearance.

The leader of the expedition was a grand sorcerer called Proudsickle. He was a strange being with haunting eyes whose mood could change from smooth charm to anger with the click of a finger.

After five wearisome years, his beard was now extremely long and the purest white. His appearance only enhanced the power of his piercing eyes. First, he looked at the grinning Grib and winced. He so despised everything the foul sommerling stood for. Then he turned within the narrow confines of the tunnel and gazed upon his other two companions. For a brief second, he smiled.

They were fools but likeable fools and had they not all been friends since their quest began back in the harsh winter of 1065?

He did enjoy the company of his favourite wizened colleague, Rumbleweed, the plump bird-lover and he knew that this expedition was the perfect way to cure his friend's broken heart. Such was the pain in Rumbleweed's heart, he knew that he would follow him into the very pits of hell. Not that he believed in hell in the Elbion sense.

"Something has gnawed my foot!" cried Rumbleweed. He waved his firebrand in a panic, sending long and macabre shadows scurrying back down the narrow passage from where they had climbed. Grib snorted in mirth at the mortal's shortcomings and deep down wished the culprit, probably a giant cave rat, had chewed off the bumbler's leg.

"Be quiet!" exclaimed Proudsickle. "It seems we now have a choice to make." He stepped to the fore with his brand and held it before him. There were two large doors before them. Amazingly, the thick wood panels and hinged brackets were as good as new.

Great cobwebs hung before them in a row after row of grey, a flimsy barrier to the secrets beyond. The smaller, hunched figure of Grib pushed the sorcerer to one side and set his brand upon the ancient shrouds. Rumbleweed saw the cobwebs catch and then suddenly vanish in a sulphurous hiss as the flame took hold. He was sure he heard the sound of scurrying above their heads and many a high-pitched scream. "That was the easy part," smiled Proudsickle. "But it fails to tell us which door to open. Do we go left or do we go right … mmm?" He turned his tall frame, which was hunched in the tight narrow passage and set his strange gaze on Bedevere, the fourth member of the party. He had also been a great magician once, had attended the great school at Garfax but now, being destitute and with the promise of discovering gold and gems, had eagerly volunteered along with Rumbleweed to uncover a lost realm hidden in the shadows of the past.

"Tell me Bedevere," purred Proudsickle in a tone of rich velvet, "Were you once the greatest at taming the third eye, didn't you once teach me?" He placed long fingers on the volunteer's shoulder. "I know you haven't lost your skills. Tell me, which is the best door to take? Which door will finally lead us to the tomb of Morgalene?"

Bedevere was the oldest of the group. He was thin, painfully so and had a straggly mane of red hair which somehow emphasized his gaunt look. Once he had been the greatest scholar at Garfax but after years of gambling and drink had lost his stature and standing. This was his last chance. Bedevere sniffed the stagnant air and then coughed.

Grib was not impressed with this fool either and thought that this mortal with his long nose and scrawny gait resembled a rat himself. "Sniff, sniff!" mocked Grib. "What will that tell us, what shall we learn?" he croaked at his own hideous mirth but was suddenly slapped across the face by Proudsickle, who gave him a withering look.

"Please, carry on dear Bedevere, what can you see?"

A grim smile crossed Bedevere's lean face. Grib frowned.

Bedevere spoke. "I was about to say the right door, yes I am certain of that. I can feel the living presence of a being beyond!"

The other three in the party looked at one another with a mixture of apprehension and excitement. The tunnel was dark and narrow with sheets of cobwebs draped across the passage like a continuous row of dank grey curtains, while the rough-hewn walls were covered in a clingy green slime which made the stomach retch. This was no place for the faint-hearted or nervous. It truly smelt of evil and death.

The four figures crept along the winding passage illuminated only by two flickering firebrands. They spoke no words for they were now weary and if truthful terrified and in awe. The way led downwards and seemed to widen but the air smelt different, not just stale but contained an odour that as yet was indistinguishable. Yet again, giant cobwebs hung from the roof to floor. When one was burned away another would be waiting. Still, the descent into the pitch-black continued. It became more slippery underfoot as patches of moss and lichen sprung up in tufts between the weathered stones.

"What an altogether foul place," gasped Rumbleweed to Bedevere, who was trailing at the end of the column. "I think our friends have led us on a fool's errand. There is no gold here just torment. Can you not smell the perfume of death?"

Grib smiled to himself, revealing his sharp teeth. "Oh, my fat jester, there will be death, of that I am sure." His words were whispered and went unheard.

Silence now engulfed the party as they continued their descent into the void. Each was consumed with their own thoughts, wondering how their lives had led them to that fearful pit. Each now wondered what horrors lay ahead. The mood of the party became as grim as their surroundings. If Proudsickle had begun the expedition with optimism and excitement, his thoughts and senses were becoming confused. He put it down to the claustrophobic atmosphere but a single doubt bothered him with each step and strained breath that they were being lured to their doom.

The air became heady once again as a musty perfume of stale flowers began to waft around them. This new sensation coincided as their descent dropped down ever more sharply and the walls closed in either side, becoming so tight that their shoulders began to scrape against the damp stone. "Here is where the shadow of death stalks," muttered Proudsickle to himself. He turned to check on his companions. His gaze was met with the heavy-lidded stare of his old grey sommerling friend. For the first time, he caught a flicker of doubt in those ancient eyes.

As Proudsickle turned to resume the journey he was greeted with a thick net of cobwebs that completely blocked their path. He held his torch and burned away the first hanging shroud only to find another and yet another barring their way. "What have you found?" called out Rumbleweed from the rear.

Proudsickle didn't respond, yet continued burning away curtain after curtain of the ancient web until eventually, his spitting flame was met with solid wood and brackets of iron. He knew they had at last found the final door. "This is the door to the tomb," gasped Bedevere. "Five long years of searching have at last come to fruition."

Grib watched in silence as the mortals became more excitable tearing away the last shrouds of web and gathering with excitement around the small door. "This is no mortal door but a sommerling hole," whispered Grib. "A final door for many a fool."

As with the previous door, this one pushed open, creaking ominously, as cobweb strands clung to the moving wood unwilling to break free from their years of bondage. The air was now putrid with the stench of stale flowers, while cobwebs surrounded and engulfed them. Those hideous strands fell before their weary eyes and were suspended above their heads. As they walked, loose strands would caress their faces even brush their lips and stroke their necks. It was almost as if they were being devoured. Firebrands were thrust forward but without effect. The webs became thicker, almost sinewy. They could hear the scurrying of light feet above their heads and now and again feel a warm breeze shake the strands, which in turn would brush their bodies. They knew they had entered a larger arena but had no idea of its shape or size.

The warm claustrophobic tunnel now gave way to an open space, instantly chilling their bones to the marrow.

Proudsickle, waved his firebrand in a large arc before him burning away the last barrier of the web. What unveiled itself took both mortal and sommerling breath away, the small door had led them through a portal to another world.

Before them was not a room or an arena, but an emptiness that knew no end.

Proudsickle gasped in awe. He compared it to the interiors of the great cathedrals of Elbion, where its giant columns of black stone, too many to count, filed away in row after row, their girth and height too enormous to understand or comprehend. Rumbleweed took a deep breath. He was now truly terrified. How he wished his old friends Tumlinfay and Sirifix were at his side. Alas, he too had chosen the wrong path. He had never felt so small or insignificant. How he wished he had stayed at his beautiful house at Greenthistle, even if he had to dwell there with a broken heart. But a broken heart will follow you anywhere, even here in the pits of doom. How he felt empty. He swallowed loudly. It was almost as if the dreaded castle was devouring his soul.

Stepping into the void, they followed the first row of giant pillars, so wide that even if the four of them linked hands they would not be able to stretch around its monstrous girth. The black stone sparkled in the pitch, as did the vaulted roof a place so distant that it could have been the very universe itself with a billion stars flickering down.

The tight cobweb-strewn passages were but a fading memory as this new world smothered them with its forbidding grandeur. But still, the party couldn't speak, they had simply lost the will to talk. This grim and foreboding castle was sucking the very life out of them, draining their will to continue. In the past, Proudsickle had committed many an evil act, as had Grib, but compared to the evil emitting from the castle's sparkling black stone and cloak of cobweb, they were nothing in the scheme of things. Their very smallness and insignificance unnerved them more than the legend of Morgalene itself.

Proudsickle waved his flickering brand. There was nothing but an overwhelming sense of emptiness. Bedevere's shaky voice came to the fore. The tone sounded strange, out of place in such a cavernous arena. Yet Proudsickle followed each word with interest. He had known the scrawny voyeur for many years, since their days at Garfax; such a wonderful gift in such a frail body. "Let us leave these pillars. Now I think it is time to touch the void!" His words were a harsh whisper. Grib sniffed repulsively and spat upon the stone floor.

Proudsickle frowned. "Go on my friend, what does your nose tell you?"

"We are not looking for a tomb my young apprentice," replied Bedevere. He smiled grimly, revealing a set of broken rotten teeth. "For we are already standing within it; Grizilder is the tomb. Can you not smell the perfume of death and decay?"

Grib sniffed. He could indeed smell death. For a brief moment, a look of doubt crept across his ugly face.

Bedevere suddenly seized a torch from Rumbleweed and turned to look at his companions. "We are near the final prize, of that I am sure. Follow me to riches beyond your imagination. Let us feast and drink from golden goblets!" He turned and swiftly vanished from view.

"Come, come," echoed his voice from the void. "We cannot keep Morgalene waiting!"

"Your mortal friend has lost his mind," croaked Grib. "What does our esteemed Proudsickle suggest now?"

The former tutor gazed into the suffocating pitch as if searching for an answer but his mind was filled with uncertainty and confusion. Here at last in the final hour of a five-year quest, he felt the strength simply drain from his legs.

"Well, oh wise one?" leered Grib, his tone mocking.

Proudsickle looked down at the loathsome sommerling, the architect of his dark thoughts and deeds. How he wished he had never drunk from the dark pool all those years ago, that he had followed another path in life. His eyes bored a hole into the sprite's foul form. How he could strike him down and be rid of him once and for all.

Grib noticed the strange expression cross Proudsickle's face and backed away further into the shadows.

"I feel we have come too far," whispered Rumbleweed. "This quest is doomed and now this accursed castle will turn us all insane."

Proudsickle composed himself. "We are but thirty yards from the greatest prize of all. "I believe Bedevere has surpassed himself."

Suddenly, there came the most gut-wrenching cry and then absolute silence. "Bedevere!" cried Rumbleweed. There came no reply. The company edged closer together and crept towards the distant flickering of Bedevere's firebrand. As the faint golden glow expanded, the full horror of their situation became slowly apparent. Bedevere was standing in silence before them, his back turned but head fixed upwards, staring in terror at this new most hideous sight.

Rising before them in that haunting dancing light was the highest throne set upon a wide circular platform of steps. The light was poor but Proudsickle, his eyes now wide with awe and terror, perceived an assortment of rounded objects at the foot, upon the sides and at the back of the high seat. While in the middle, on the seat of the gruesome chair, was an enormous bundle of black rags. Grib and Proudsickle edged closer while Bedevere and Rumbleweed stood shivering with a fear so great they almost collapsed in terror.

Grib's long clawed fingers scraped upon the first row of domed objects.

He now knew he was caressing skulls, faery or human, he couldn't tell. Even his dark mind tried hard to absorb this new terrifying sight. Proudsickle followed closely behind, dragging his heavy cloak on up the steps. His mind too was filled with grim thoughts, as if all light and fairness had finally left him never to return. The ancient skulls were grimacing back in macabre smiles, there must have been a thousand at least decorated around the throne, a throne of death and despair. Grib was the first to reach the giant cluster of rags. Why they were stacked there from the top of the chair billowing down to the floor, he couldn't tell. He turned and beckoned Bedevere and Rumbleweed to follow. Upon the arm of the chair was placed a large silver goblet. He bent to look inside and even he, the foulest sommerling of them all, recoiled in disgust. The liquid inside had almost set. He dipped his hairy finger inside and felt its stodgy coldness. "Must be a wine of some sort," he croaked to himself. Grib took the cup, which at first resisted, clinging to its resting place with a foul green substance and then pretended to drink from it. Soon his little joke became maniacal as he screeched out loud and began dancing before the pile of rags.

The others looked on in disgust. "He really is a despicable little fellow," seethed Rumbleweed. "He will attract bad luck and ill fortune."

Proudsickle looked on at the bizarre scene remembering the dark pool all those years ago and his unfortunate seduction. He knew that they had got it wrong, badly so. There was no wealth, no secrets, just a stained silver goblet and the mad jig of a dancing sommerling. Yet a power he did not yet understand kept him entranced. There was a wealth of some sort, he could feel the excitement beginning to course through his veins, yet there was no obvious sign of it. It was a puzzle he didn't understand.

"Shall we give the queen a drink," hissed the sommerling to the rags. He climbed nimbly upon the arm of the high chair and tilted the goblet to where an unseen head might have been, all the time laughing and screeching.

The sorcerer looked up in contempt. He had never witnessed such an awful sight. He really would have to cancel the agreement and kill the sommerling once and for all.

Just then, amid the dancing flames and hideous cackles, a single drop of liquid fell from the goblet upon the crumpled, black rags. The green liquid hissed as if burning the material. Grib continued to pour the liquid over the cloth, until suddenly, where once the black material was gathered, there became exposed the largest most hideous skull, still sprouting threads of white hair. The long hair now fell freely over the sides of the throne. Grib became rooted to the spot with the goblet tilted over the exposed head. They had found Morgalene at last!

Rumbleweed fled from the steps in horror while Bedevere and Proudsickle baulked and then began walking slowly backwards, their hearts beating ever faster.

Another drop fell upon the skull then dripped down upon the long-beaked nose. Grib stood transfixed at the unfolding scene. The liquid then slowly fell from the tip of the hideous nose and down the bared teeth of the monstrous skull.

"What have you done, you fool!" cried Bedevere.

First, one eye socket clicked open. It couldn't see yet though it could sense its surroundings. After all those long, long years, life had returned to her; oh joy but oh the hunger, the terrible hunger!

Grib jumped from the throne as soon as he saw the

head begin to turn, sending the goblet and its foul contents crashing to the floor below; yet Bedevere had strayed too near. He was bewitched at the magic before him. Suddenly, a long sinewy arm thrust out from the falling rags and grabbed the scrawny magician around the throat, crushing his neck and then began to drag his limp body upwards to the high throne and the very jaws of Morgalene herself.

4

Memories of a Witch

WHAT scenes followed on from poor Bedevere's death are hard to imagine. Morgalene's hunger had, for the moment, been slaked.

Proudsickle and Grib gazed up in enchantment mixed with horror as the witch began to change before their very eyes. Luminous white skin began to grow around her massive skull, covering the bone and bulbous veins alike. Her white hair now darkened until it was black, the front streak of dyed red remaining.

After her replenishment, Morgalene sat back and inspected her hands, which in truth were just long-nailed claws. She smiled gruesomely for in her disturbed mind, she was but a beautiful princess again.

Her poor vision was not matched by her sharp sense of smell. She could not see the intruders clearly but she could smell their blood, two tasty morsels quivering before her just waiting to be eaten!

She moved her aching bulk from side to side, this, in turn, sent two ancient skulls, crashing and clattering down the steps landing directly at the feet of Proudsickle and Grib. As the sorcerers looked down, they could see the hollowed smiles gazing up at them in a macabre greeting.

Proudsickle and Grib looked at one another in growing horror and doubt. Maybe they should have fled back into the dark vaults with Rumbleweed. Then the awful voice of Morgalene broke the silence. As her jaw opened, clicking loudly with each movement, so saliva dropped to the cold stone below. She shook her vast cloak sending a cloud of dust into the already stifling air.

The harsh voice was in faery, an ancient variety, yet both mortal and sommerling understood.

"Who are you to wake me, little men?" she asked mockingly. "Do you know who I am?"

Proudsickle bowed, as did Grib, who for once was truly terrified.

"Speak!" She roared, sending more skulls crashing to the ground. A droplet of green saliva from the witch splashed across the face of Proudsickle. It was the sorcerer who spoke first while dabbing his face with a handkerchief.

"We thought it time to awake you, your majesty," he replied confidently. Grib looked up at him and sneered.

Morgalene then reared up from the throne, pulled up her vast swathes of black cloth and in one bizarre, truly terrifying moment, descended the steps and brought her extremely ugly countenance face to face with Proudsickle, her nose but an inch from his own.

Still he didn't flinch, yet Grib took two steps back.

Proudsickle could now smell her odour of death and decay. He coughed, while Grib cowered, waiting for death to follow. But death did not follow, instead, something unexpected happened.

"Dragool, is it you my sweet?" Morgalene stared at the tall sorcerer and sniffed the air. "You have come back for me after all these years!" she exclaimed, her voice softening, yet still hideous to behold.

Proudsickle stood firm as the foul breath of the witch wafted over him.

"I am Dragool, your majesty," he replied calmly, "And I have indeed come back for you."

Grib was impressed with his old rival's bravery and stopped cowering.

The witch had been placated. Her huge mouth closed and the saliva stopped dripping.

"Mmmph," she snorted, looking Proudsickle up and down. Despite her poor vision, the figure before her was familiar with sound and scent. "You seem different, taller maybe. You always were the only one who didn't grovel in my presence, always so strong."

Morgalene twisted her boil-ridden neck and suddenly thrust her face before Grib. "Who is your ugly friend?" Her teeth began to grind, she was not impressed with this hunched dwarf, though obviously of bad blood, a sommerling from the shadows, maybe a useful plaything.

"He is called the Grib, my queen," answered the

sorcerer, trying not to smirk. "He is my most valuable assistant."

The sprite glowered in anger, then let out a sneeze, as particles of ancient dust tickled his long nose.

Morgalene smiled and in one swift movement turned and lifting up her black rags as if she were a maiden at a spring ball, climbed back up the long steps to the comfort of her throne.

"I wish to sleep now," she croaked. "Leave me for now but fetch me some wine upon your return."

With that, her enormous figure slumped down, her head disappearing into the folds of her rags leaving her long black hair to drop down the arms of the throne to the floor below.

In the shadows, Proudsickle and Grib talked in harsh whispers hoping their voices would not wake the sleeping monster.

"Dragool," hissed Grib. "More fool, if you ask me."

"As you know I studied the legend of Morgalene at university many years ago," replied Proudsickle. "I believe this Dragool was her personal sorcerer, as was written in those ancient manuscripts."

Grib frowned as a maniacal smile crossed the sorcerer's smug face.

"This is the only reason we are alive," added Proudsickle, "Morgalene must think that I have risen from a deathly slumber too."

Suddenly, they both jumped, as the witch let out a hideous snore and an ominous grinding of large teeth.

"Look, I know we have fallen out over the last fifty years and I'm sure that you wish me dead," said the sorcerer, his voice hushed and fast.

"You've guessed!" laughed Grib, "Nothing personal."

"But we have to court favour, one slip-up and we are both dead," said Proudsickle. "Let us do her bidding for now and we will emerge as victors, do you agree?"

Two hours later, though the dark was misleading, two trembling figures were standing before the throne, one carrying a tray, which held a goblet and a flagon of foul-smelling liquid. Grib never explained how he came by it but the discovery extended their lives.

Morgalene stirred and she opened her eyes. She could make out the two figures below, though her watery eyes were rheumy with age.

Her brief sleep had brought back many memories. She wondered how long she had slept. Despite her poor vision, she could see the tall sorcerer Dragool standing loyally before her, his fingers turning his tall hat over and over in his hands. A habit he had retained after all those years.

As for the other creature, so like the goblin-sommerlings that used to pull her cloak from behind as she walked the battlements of Grizilder, she could sense his impure heart. She would have to watch that one closely, for he was too good to kill for now.

Her claws tensed while the atmosphere in the grim arena tingled.

The witch's dreams had tormented her dark soul, they cut like a poisoned knife. Her mind darkened and then in an instant, she understood. Rosewene had awoken! She could hear her sister's voice in her head, gasping that her true love was coming once again for her, to escape from the gardens of Liminulin.

"Yes," pondered Morgalene to herself. "So that was where the elf-fool Eldsmoreth took you in his arms before he abandoned you to flee north." She remembered it so clearly now as her legions of sommerlings hunted the elf down; the sword and the walking stick.

Grib coughed loudly and spat to the ground.

Morgalene stopped reminiscing and craned her long neck forward, glaring with ferocity at the reckless sommerling, a blackened sprite, she guessed. "Good move," growled Proudsickle through gritted teeth.

Morgalene returned to her position and smiled down at Grib. The fouler the better, she thought.

Suddenly, Morgalene let out a terrifying scream, forcing Proudsickle and Grib to cover their ears. Skulls of all varieties were sent crashing to the floor in every direction.

The witch slumped in her seat, claws covering her ugly face.

"I only spat," croaked Grib nervously to the sorcerer.

"Rosewene is awake!" she cried, her words echoing

around the chamber. "Then if she has awoken she can destroy me!" Her thin voice then faded, she did not want to appear weak.

But Proudsickle had heard the words clearly and his mind worked fast. "Rosewene, your majesty?" enquired the sorcerer gravely, while he fingered his pointed hat. "Has she been discovered?"

Proudsickle and Grib stayed with Morgalene for twenty-one days to be exact. No one knows for certain what food they found to eat, or what wine was consumed but endure they did and prosper too. And so, if it were possible, two dark souls became darker and more knowledgeable. Proudsickle played the role of Dragool perfectly while Grib the loyal servant.

At first, they played their roles for survival but then Morgalene began sharing her knowledge, wittingly and unwittingly and increased their power thus opening up a new and sinister world of possibilities.

Morgalene soon learned of Gilindon's demise (Elbion's ancient name) and the ending of the age of sommerling.

She listened as the sorcerer's hypnotic words washed over her and would suddenly gasp and gurgle if she heard something unexpected. She was but a child listening to a tale. Even Grib was amazed at what Prousdsickle had to say.

She then heard how over the many centuries the island was resettled, reborn into the land of Elbion, a mortal land soft and plump, now ready to conquer and of course Proudsickle would lead the way for her!

Not once did she question how he knew all of this, much to Grib's relief. The answers to the past were in the ancient sommerling manuscripts salvaged from Garfax's fire and were safely locked away at Proudsickle's home at Grendeline.

5

The Rose Fayre

TRIFAN slowly opened his eyes, tentatively he stretched his toes sensing for a frost that was not there.

In the distance, he could hear the sound of song and laughter and then a high chime of the church bell. As his head began to clear, it was obvious that the snows had belonged to a terrible dream. A soft ray of sunlight now bathed his face as it crept through the open window of his room within the castle tower.

Quickly, he threw back his bedsheets, pulled on his best green tunic and soft brown trousers and went to the window.

He could see below that Oakendale was busy preparing itself for the first day of the Rose Fayre. The clear bell chimed once more. The last late trader had been granted permission to enter the meadow. A sudden gust of excitement swept over him as he looked down at the vast spectacle of moving colour, smells and noise. It was the only time in the year that Oakendale would awake from its own comfortable slumber. From his vantage point, he had a good view of the large church meadow which had filled out with travellers. Each erected tent, of which there were hundreds, all brightly dyed in their own elaborate styles, now bordered the tree-lined perimeter. He wondered which one belonged to that strange, yet pleasant, Mr Tumlinfay.

After tidying the garden, Trifan scoffed down a quick breakfast of oatcakes and milk from the kitchens and then, with a whistle on his lips, made his way to the church meadow determined to make the most of his day off.

The first day of the Rose Fayre attracted not only the eager and excited inhabitants of the town but also folk from every corner of Elbion. It transformed Oakendale's usually peaceful existence into a mass of rumbling carts and noisy travellers. There were over a thousand folks swarming around the Fayre. They came from Camelon and Northfolk; these were mostly thatchers, crofters, weavers and clothmakers.

There was a large following of gypsies from Elona and blacksmiths with armour, horseshoes and nails.

There were potters and craftsmen from Fluxen and Weffolk, fishmongers with that morning's early catch from the River Freshbright, wine and cider merchants from the gentle slopes of Eaffolk and hop-growers from as far away as Cent, selling their special brands of ale known throughout the kingdom, and even abroad, as Canterbrooks Strong Bitter and Southern Surprise. There were knights, representing each shire of the realm, their valets and a group of druids from Webbenden, not to mention the throng of visitors and bargain hunters, filling the meadow to bursting point. It was no surprise that just after nine o'clock in the morning the wardens of the church declared the Rose Fayre full for the first day's trading. Once inside the meadow, Trifan found himself engulfed within a sea of colour and spectacle. Bright tapestries adorned the many stalls and colourful banners were draped from the oak trees that lined the edge of that large field. There was noise and bustle everywhere as people young and old, rich and poor, thronged to the stalls that caught their eye.

Trifan was swept along in a tide of jostling bodies, as stallholders shouted each other down in a cacophony of noise.

There were almost two hundred stalls, selling everything from chain mail, hoes, pots, pans, pies, ale, cheeses, clay pipes and birdseed. Despite the heat and an almost endless onslaught of flies and insects, the good folk of Oakendale were determined to have a good day.

Amid this chaos Trifan found his two friends, Edwyn Bracey and Tervy Shrew, stealing apples and tying boot-laces together. He had to laugh aloud when the two youths were apprehended by a friar of the Abbey, Brother Orsam and were dragged squealing to their feet by their ears.

"Ah, good morning!" said the large friar upon seeing

Trifan. "Keeping out of trouble I see, unlike your friends here. If they step out of line again, I shall have no hesitation in bringing them swiftly back within the Abbey walls, shaving their heads once more into tonsures and putting them to work scrubbing the kitchen floors and tending my cabbages."

Brother Orsam had been not only a friend to Trifan but also a father figure. He had brought the boy into the care of the church when he was orphaned as a two-year-old. He had even found him lodgings within the castle and a job in the Royal Rose-Gardens when he had left the harsh but protective arms of the Abbey. That had been two years ago when Trifan had been a very troublesome fourteen-year-old.

"I'd hoped that I helped put them back upon the correct path to righteousness," said Brother Orsam, finally letting go.

"Don't worry, I think you've taught them enough religious studies for one day," replied Trifan laughing loudly.

"When I say enjoy the fayre lads, I mean try keeping out of mischief," grumbled the Friar. He then turned, unsmiling and shifted his bulk into the throng of fayregoers, quickly disappearing from view.

"What's the matter with him?" asked Trifan, curious at the Friar's tetchiness.

"I don't know," answered Edwyn as he rubbed his ear. "He hasn't been the same since he saw the flying dragon the other night."

"I don't think anyone believes him," added Tervy, "They say he had drunk too much wine."

"I could still smell it on his breath," winced Edwyn, "Along with eggs."

"Well I believe him," replied Trifan, a little too swiftly.

"If you ask me you've been working in the sun too long", laughed Edwyn. "Surely you don't believe in dragons whether they are flying or sleeping."

"It's getting so bad I've heard the King is sending his guard from Flax to protect the southern shires," added Tervy.

"From what?" scoffed Edwyn.

"From wandering demons and sommerlings," said Tervy, the youngest and more believing of all the tales from the taverns.

Edwyn slapped the smaller boy on the back, "Come on, enough of this. I'm off for a dip in the river, it's getting too hot for me."

"I think I'll join you," said Tervy, who was already sweating under his coarse tunic.

"Are you coming, Trif...?" asked Edwyn.

"No, not yet, I've come here to see someone," replied Trifan hesitantly.

"What's her name, then?" laughed Tervy, winking at Edwyn.

"It's not Alison, the old maid's daughter?" smirked the older boy.

"Definitely not!" said Trifan his face reddening. "It's someone else, a traveller of great importance."

"Who then?" said his friends together.

"Oh, only the Dragon, of course, he has asked me over," answered Trifan with a grin. "Look, give me an hour and I'll join you in the river."

His friends looked on baffled as Trifan vanished into the crowd.

"First Orsam, now Trifan. Things are getting stranger by the day," remarked Edwyn, scratching his head.

"I wonder what he's up to. If I wasn't so hot, I would follow him," added Tervy, "I told you he's turning into a younger version of Grimridge."

After much searching, Trifan finally found the stall that Mr Tumlinfay had claimed for himself. Already it had a throng of people gathered around it, all thoroughly impressed by this new travelling sorcerer. His magic and trickery drew many a gasp of astonishment and a round of cheers. He produced two doves from under his broad hat that immediately flew into the sky and plucked eggs from his mouth that suddenly cracked and hatched into tiny chicks. As well as these various acts of disappearance and deception he showed them mind-bending charts of the stars and revealed their secrets, he demonstrated potions with cures for backache, colds, stomach pains, headaches and hangovers. Whatever the growing crowd requested he would duly oblige them and, in many cases, cure them. In the middle of the second show, just after eleven, Tumlinfay looked up and saw Trifan standing amongst the crowd of onlookers.

"Well, well, if it isn't the keeper of the gardens!" said the old man, his blue eyes twinkling under bushy, white brows.

Trifan felt awkward as the crowd turned curiously to look at him. "I'm terribly sorry," said Tumlinfay addressing the crowd loudly. "But I shall be closing for an early lunch. Please come back, later."

And with that, he stood up swiftly and placed a large 'Closed' sign at the front of his stall. The crowd looked on in surprise and then turned away muttering and moaning under their breath.

"Miserable bunch," murmured the old man as he beckoned the boy over. "Come join me, young fellow, let us share a pipe together."

They spent the rest of the afternoon chatting about travel, trickery and the garden. All the time Tumlinfay looked keenly at the boy. Trifan marvelled at the old man's knowledge concerning all matters, especially regarding flora and fauna and in particular gardening.

So entrenched were they that Trifan failed to notice the oncoming sunset and the realisation that the Fayre had long since packed up for the evening. Shadows were by now cast over the church meadow, leaving only the pale lights of tradesmen's lanterns to pierce the gloom, like many will-o'-the-wisps. The smell of cooking drifted into the hot night air mingling with the joyful sounds of singing and merry-making. Tumlinfay listened with pleasure to the songs and leaned back upon the trunk of an oak. His face was shadowed under his broad-rimmed hat, while his eyes glistened like two bright stars. It felt to Trifan as though the old man was studying him. The feeling made him a little uneasy.

"Where do you come from?" queried Trifan after a long, awkward silence. "My home lies to the south, in Fluxen," he answered. "Half a day's flying. I trust you are still looking after my dragon?"

"You didn't come to Oakendale for the Fayre, did you?"

Trifan's remark surprised even himself and he wondered why he had said it. "My, my, you are indeed a perceptive man for one so young," replied Tumlinfay looking surprised. "Yes, I am visiting Oakendale on other matters. But the annual Rose Fayre is somewhere that I have always wanted to visit. Its reputation throughout the kingdom is second to none, don't you know. I thought it a chance of bringing a little magic and culture to the northern shires!"

"You certainly brought that," replied Trifan smiling. "I found your show very entertaining. You're the talk of Oakendale by now, though I'm not suggesting that you're weird to look at."

"That's what I had intended," said Tumlinfay stroking his perfectly pointed, white beard. "But I still make babies cry and old women tremble!" With the help of his walking stick, Tumlinfay clambered to his feet and gazed upward to the stars. Then he turned and looked sharply at Trifan.

"I am searching for someone, or should I say, searching for a lady. I believe she resides nearby." Tumlinfay smiled, he so enjoyed teasing the boy.

Trifan shrugged his shoulders. Oakendale was, despite being the shire's largest town, a fairly small, tight-knit place. "What's her name maybe I know her?"

"She is called Rosewene, my friend," replied Tumlinfay with a touch of fondness in his voice. "It is most important that I find her and find her soon."

"I wish I could help," offered Trifan. "She has a strange name – it sounds sort of old."

"It is an old name," said Tumlinfay. "But enough of this, we have talked all afternoon and much of the night. It is your bedtime now and I have a busy day ahead tomorrow, if the citizens of Oakendale have forgiven me. I trust you will be popping over to the Fayre again?"

"Yes of course," answered Trifan enthusiastically, "I haven't enjoyed myself so much in ages."

"That is good," said Tumlinfay smiling. "I have enjoyed talking to you, especially about your beautiful rose gardens. It has been most enlightening." He held out a hand and clasped Trifan's wrist. "Well goodnight for now and sweet dreams." He smiled once more then turned away with a heavy yawn. Trifan watched the magician retire to his tent and then departed the meadow and crossed over Barnyard's Lane, his mind still racing with all

Tumlinfay had shown him. That night he went to bed with the strange name of Rosewene upon his lips.

The old man certainly had more up his sleeve than he was letting on. It was as if he was holding something back. His genial eyes held a secret that for now would not be revealed.

Tumlinfay remained at the Rose Fayre throughout the three days, encamped behind his stall in the far corner of the meadow, alongside the other traders' various lodgings.

Whenever Trifan had time off from work, depending on the mood of Grimridge, he would go down to the church meadow and help Tumlinfay set up a stall with a seemingly endless supply of new tricks. How he came by such items was a mystery to Trifan. Whenever he turned up in the morning, before the opening of the Fayre, he would have them out by the tent waiting to be set in place: new tricks, games, illusions, crystal-balls, magic-mirrors, strange drawings and an endless supply of doves, rabbits, frogs and chicks. They appeared as if by magic. From where they came, Tumlinfay wouldn't say. He would simply smile and pat Trifan upon the head.

Early the following morning, Trifan was toiling away on a small, untended plot at the south end of the garden. He mopped his sweat-stained brow and thought about ending his unfulfilling toil, even though he had only been working for about an hour or so. A trip down to the meadow to see his mysterious new friend seemed to be the order of the day.

As he gazed down at the weed-covered patch he realised that there was more to life than being a gardener. He suddenly wished he was working elsewhere, like the Royal Stables perhaps. Maybe one day he would be a knight of Elbion, riding around the countryside, jousting, or seeking lost treasure. Or maybe Tumlinfay would take him on as an apprentice. After all, he had no ties in Oakendale, no family. For a stinging moment, he felt very much alone.

But the thought intrigued him, as he saw himself with Tumlinfay, floating up into the sky, in that ugly contraption of his, drifting up amongst the clouds into new lands and adventure.

But no, he was still slaving in the garden and weeding the beds. Just then, as he was digging into the soil, his trowel hit against something hard. There was a loud clink of metal touching metal. For a moment, he forgot his daydreams and began to use his hands to clear the remainder of loose soil from around the object; which in turn revealed a glimmer of exposed silver as soon as the earth had been removed. A chink of brilliance suddenly dazzled him sharply in the eye.

Little by little, Trifan uncovered the object and soon managed to wrench it free from its shallow resting place. "Well, well, what have we here?" he murmured. "How beautiful is this."

The object was a strange-looking sword, long and sleek, which measured about four feet in length. It was unlike any sword he had ever seen before. As the light from the blade reflected upon Trifan's face, the rich glow seemed to beguile him in its warmth and beauty. "How strange," he mused, "I've worked on this plot last summer and all I came across were stones and worms. I suppose it must have belonged to someone in the castle. Whoever owned it must have been important."

His first thought was to inform the castle guards of his find. There was bound to be a reward for it. But then, as he looked down at his discovery and saw the strange light reaching out to him, touching his skin, he thought otherwise.

Quickly, he tucked the sword under the swirls of his baggy tunic and pressed it close to his body, feeling strangely exhilarated, yet at the same time like a thief in the night.

"You are beautiful," he whispered, "I know just the place to hide you away." The blade warmed to his body.

Clutching the sword closer to his chest, he quickly made his way to the old potting shed. Once inside its dark confines, he placed the sword upon the potting bench, under the curious gaze from a large spider's web. He stood back from it and watched, almost half-expecting it to suddenly glow once more. But nothing happened: its warm light had dimmed to grey.

It looked to Trifan as if it were sleeping. "Rest here for

now," he whispered. He then covered the sword under a clean table- cloth and left the shed, locking it behind him as he went and so hurried on toward the meadow. Trifan spent the remainder of the day helping Mr Tumlinfay on his stall, which still proved to be one of the most popular attractions at the Fayre. If he wasn't setting up maps and props, he was chasing the many small animals that kept escaping, much to the amusement of the large crowd.

He kept news of his find secret and that included all of his friends and Mr Tumlinfay. Whether it was his imagination, he had an uneasy feeling that the old magician was studying him again. On the outside, Tumlinfay appeared friendly and easy-going, almost like an uncle he never had but whenever he spoke of work or the garden, in particular, a strange expression would cross the magician's face.

Later that night, after another hectic day at the Fayre, Trifan returned to the gloom of the potting shed, having decided to check up on the beautiful sword He pulled away from the cloth and looked down upon its form. "You are indeed fair to look upon," he sighed. "You shall be safe with me now." He suddenly realised that he was talking to himself. He picked up the sword and immediately felt at ease. Without a second thought, he began waving the weapon in the air, fencing with an unseen foe. But as he was about to slice open a soil bag, he suddenly felt a searing pain run up his arm. He cried out in agony and dropped the sword to the floor, with a loud clang.

Within the darkness of the shed, the gloom began to give way to a golden glimmer, which radiated out from the sword. At first, Trifan felt like running away but something made him stay. The mysterious glow suddenly grew, reaching upward to the beamed roof. Half-shielding his eyes from the haunting light, he could see its strange magic unveiling in all its glory, binding him closer to its warmth, drawing him in, until he felt as one with the sword. In an instant, Trifan could see many visions flash before his eyes, new sights appear then disappear. At first, he could see a great castle with many turrets reaching for darkened skies and below its edifice, he saw a garden, in which grew many wondrous flowering trees and plants. Amidst this beauty he saw a young maiden dance, she was twisting and turning like a leaf upon a soft autumn breeze. Her white dress billowed around her slender waist, while her fair hair flowed under a crown of yellow flowers but all the time her face remained hidden from view. Then the bright light began to fade, eaten away by encroaching darkness until the castle and the garden and then the maiden finally vanished from view. Trifan stood absolutely still, in shock and awe. He breathed deeply, trying to understand the magic before his eyes. After gathering his thoughts, he quickly replaced the cloth over the sword, as one would cover a sleeping child. He then placed his discovery in a safe hiding place, before locking the shed and hurrying home to his bed. "What does it all mean?" he murmured aloud, as he climbed the many stairs leading to his lodgings. "An enchanted sword, nobody would ever believe me!" he gasped. "My friends will think I am mad. Who am I to tell?"

When Trifan eventually fell asleep that night, he dreamt of the dancing maiden with fair hair, this time he could see her face and it was enchanting, unlike any woman he had ever seen before. He was standing before her in a grove of ancient trees and tall ferns. She held his hand and led him to the largest tree. There she swept aside a curtain of ivy, revealing to him a door, fixed against the broad trunk.

"You do have the key?" she asked urgently and in panic before she too began to vanish from view. In the morning he remembered nothing of the dream, though he could smell the scent of the forest on his pillow and it was a scent that beguiled him.

The third and last day of the Rose Fayre was one of the hottest spring days in living memory for the citizens of Oakendale. All serious attempts to complete a full day of trading began to fade around two o'clock, as the sun reached its peak. Almost half the church meadow was now empty, as traders, fortune-tellers, gypsies, actors, knights and tinkers departed with exasperation, on the long pilgrimage home, to their various shires of the kingdom.

Soon, Barnyard's Lane, was one long, dust-ridden column, of rumbling carts, colour, noise, driven beasts, riders and people on foot; a large village on the move. For those who remained, there was a scant respite from the heat. All the ale-houses in the vicinity were empty of all wines and beers. The River Freshbright, which during the course of the month, had dropped to its lowest level for fifty years, was filled with hundreds of naked, flailing and thrashing bodies, all seeking pleasure from its fleeting relief. There was nothing to do except retreat to the shade.

By late afternoon, the meadow was empty, save for a few local stall-holders packing their remaining unsold goods onto carts.

Despite trying conditions, the annual Rose Fayre had been a major success. The church had reclaimed its much-trampled meadow and the Abbot was gleefully counting his share of the profits. For the remainder of the year, the rich meadow would be used as grazing for horses, ponies and sheep.

Within the tall, green-hedged borders there was an unusual silence. The only reminder of the preceding, hectic days was the lingering odours of stale ale, crushed grass and manure.

All was calm upon the greensward, except in a far corner of the meadow where Trifan, who had been helping Tumlinfay for most of the morning, now helped pack up some of the old man's belongings into a small trunk. Most of his other tricks and maps he had given away, saying that he now had little use for them.

"You're welcome to change your mind about leaving," insisted Trifan, knowing that the old magician would soon be on his way. "If you want, I could put you up in lodgings within the castle. Most rooms are vacant now the Royal Household has moved to Flax."

"The generosity is much appreciated young man," replied Tumlinfay. "But I have other errands to run, other paths to follow. Do not worry, I shall return to Oakendale one day, maybe on a day when you have forgotten all about me."

Tumlinfay never did discuss his errands, or what they entailed. His movements, like his many varied tricks, remained a mystery. If Trifan ever asked any questions the magician would simply smile and pat him on the head, before remarking. "Such questions have no easy answers, just enjoy the sun and keep out of trouble!"

At the old man's request, Trifan gave him a tour of the vast rose gardens before his departure. There, amid the heavily scented flowers and infinite colours, Tumlinfay gazed around in child-like wonder. He took off his hat, as if in reverence and stared fondly at Trifan. If perhaps, you should meet Rosewene," said Tumlinfay, "look after her for me until I return."

"When will you return?" asked Trifan confused, but pleased he might after all be seeing the old man again.

"When you least expect me," replied the magician with a smile. "But soon, I hope, for I have a journey to make and a very important letter to write." That night, in the dull, humid surroundings of the garden, everything appeared sombre, as Tumlinfay and his strange flying contraption floated up into the sky, belching flames like a large, bloated dragon.

His gradual disappearance felt to Trifan like the passing of a dream. The mysterious, old man departed from Oakendale with a lot less fuss than when he had arrived. Trifan smiled as he remembered how only a few days earlier, he had looked on in horror as the magician had crash-landed upon his most prized bed of roses.

Soon, Tumlinfay and his creation were disappearing out of sight. Trifan wiped a tear from his eye and wondered if he would ever see the old magician again.

6

Morgalene's Box

AFTER Tumlinfay's departure from Oakendale, the magician returned to his home at Golenwood which lay to the south, upon the borders of Whitewebbs Forest.

From his study, he composed a long, encrypted letter to his one-time rival, the Grand Wizard himself, who happened to dwell in the east, also upon the borders of that great wood.

Within the letter, he confirmed his discovery and his contact with Trifan. At first, even before he had lowered his nib into the ink, he had a niggling doubt. But as the enormity of his task unfolded in his mind, he quickly put pen to paper. Proudsickle was, after all, head of the order and had to be afforded respect, despite their mutual mistrust and subsequent falling out. It was his first letter in over five years.

Before the week was up, Tatia, the magician's most trustworthy of doves, had successfully avoided the hawks and owls of northern Whitewebbs and arrived within the luxurious study at Grendeline Manor, with the urgent message strapped to its back.

Proudsickle, fresh from his secret trip to Mortenden only a few months before, was sitting by the open window waiting to receive it. The white dove had done well but was nervous and for good reason. The sorcerer's long, nimble fingers unfastened the small wicker box from Tatia's back and unfurled the parchment, that Tumlinfay had penned in miniature. Two enormous magpies cackled and croaked while resting upon the sorcerer's shoulders. The sorcerer smiled down at the timid bird. "My dear Tarak and Belbar, show our guest to her lodgings, I'm sure she needs the rest!" Both birds dropped down to the table, hopping over to the dove's side. But the weary Tatia could only sense her impending doom. Suddenly, free of her cumbersome box, she fluttered frantically from the open window, taking all by surprise, heading desperately for the cover of the forest.

Proudsickle clicked his finger and soon Tarak and the ugly Belbar were falling upon their prey in the garden beyond, killing her swiftly and without mercy. "So, Tumlinfay," he spoke aloud. "You are bored in retirement are you and wish to rejoin your brothers in the Order." He smiled smugly, pleased that he was still respected. "Of course you can return, especially now as we are two down."

Proudsickle leant back in his leather chair and with his

crystal glasses, deciphered the hundred or so words. The words were tiny but they cut like a poisoned knife.

Suddenly, he screamed with uncontrollable rage and leapt from his seat. Striding to the sunlit window, he slammed them shut and drew the heavy, embroidered curtains. The lone flickering flame of a large candle illuminated his tense, sweat-streaked face. His eyes bored into Tumlinfay's words. He wondered if he was going mad. How did this wandering magician get involved? He was meant to be skulking in the countryside in his house by the woods. He knew he should have invited this meddler upon the great quest those five winters past. But didn't a voice in his head say no? There was always something strange about Tumlinfay, a puzzle he couldn't solve. Fate could prove so cruel.

"So, my over-inquisitive friend, you have the answer to my dreams in your palm. My, how you have upstaged me! You always were a dramatic, yet secret fellow." Proudsickle's mind darkened. How he had travelled down his own lonely road, for fifty years, ever since his enchantment and rebirth in the dark pool. Old acquaintances and bonds would count for nothing. Tumlinfay would have to be destroyed. His mind began to race, as this new gift appeared to offer itself. He wiped spittle from the corners of his mouth and smiled. "Maybe, you were meant to unearth the elves but my destiny is to possess them! You discovered Rosewene and Eldsmoreth and I awoke Morgalene! You have played your part well, dear Tumlinfay." He spoke the words aloud, as the last trace of sanity began to leave him. The dark pool had won, as it always did. "Then I shall pay a visit to the secret rose garden and see for myself this upstart serf, Trifan. Then we shall bury him in his own plot and take dear Rosewene and Eldsmoreth." He looked down at Tumlinfay's final words. "Of course, you fool, you want me to send messages to our diminishing order," he chuckled darkly. "Well, Bedevere is with Morgalene now, as is dear Rumbleweed." The sorcerer chortled to himself as he remembered how he had coaxed his old companion toward the throne of Morgalene. "And I won't bother Mordegan, quite sensibly a recluse and Windlesax, well, too old and nervous for a task such as this. There, my dear Tumlinfay, I've sent my mail. The Gathering of the Order will be such a quiet affair!"

A large bird suddenly appeared at the sorcerer's side.

"Tarak, my dear magpie, so Belbar is still feasting?" The hideous bird cackled malevolently.

"Then Oakendale it is," announced Proudsickle. "Such a pretty place if I remember. Tarak, fetch me a map of the northern shires, for I have a journey to make."

Proudsickle knew the moment had come. He smiled, for though he had descended so far into madness and evil, his mind had to remain clear for such an important task, simple though it was. "Ah, Morgalene's gift, yes of course, how could I forget." He arose from his chair, left the study and unlatched a small door that led off the large entrance hallway. He lit a candle, descended the twenty-two cold steps, until he had entered a broad cellar, with a curved ceiling. With his long gown, brushing the stone floor, he moved purposefully to a dark corner, which housed a high rack, containing two-hundred, or so, bottles of fine Aluivian red wine. His long, nimble fingers, swept aside the fast woven cobwebs, that had threaded across some of the older bottles until they reached out into a deep recess and touched upon an ancient and very long, wooden box, a wondrous gift from his new beautiful queen.

Sighing with pleasure, he pulled it free, studying the strangely carved runes that decorated its entire length. Chuckling darkly, he eagerly opened the ugly box. Set inside were nine bulbous bottles. It was not what he expected, in truth. Six bottles contained a liquid of the purest white, two bottles were grey, while the last, was a sickly green. The temptation to open one was great but he resisted, remembering the harsh words of his queen only a few weeks before. If opened, his throat would be ripped apart and his flesh feasted upon. He had to save this gift for Oakendale and for the foolish keeper of Rosewene. For, whatever spirits dwelt within would be drawn to the sword and walking stick. "Three chances to slay, white, then grey, with green to follow." He chuckled at the witch's little rhyme. Morgalene was sure to reward him now. How they would sweep all before their path. How his power had grown. Ha! He closed the box carefully and then ascended the damp cellar steps, muttering to himself as he went.

7

The Secret of the Rose-Garden

OVER a month had passed since Tumlinfay's departure from Oakendale and life went back to normal for Trifan. He would rise from his bed at seven and work through to about five in the afternoon. His evenings were spent with his friends, fishing, or swimming in the River Freshbright, or visiting either the Black Bull or Unicorn Inn, listening to numerous tales of strange happenings from travellers journeying up from the south. Some nights he would visit Friar Orsam, in his herb garden and sit with him under the stars, talking and sharing a tankard of ale.

Still, he had seen no sign of this Rosewene. He didn't even know what this lady looked like. Tumlinfay had been very short on detail. Maybe she was an old girlfriend, a heart he had once broken on his travels. Perhaps the old magician was confused, he did seem a little eccentric.

Trifan enjoyed visiting the Unicorn most of all. Every

night a new collection of weathered wandering folk would rest for a meal and a drink and converse with the locals. Many had spent long, arduous days, hiking, or hitching upon carriages and carts. That particular night, a family had travelled up from Mallowden, the weary children were now fast asleep in the guest house, while the father, a blacksmith from Rye, told of a silent and abandoned shire, where at night sommerling-demons came hunting. Trifan shivered as the man recounted a tale of slaughtered sheep and missing children. "But, where will you go?" asked Tapwine the landlord.

The blacksmith looked up at him with wide eyes. "We are travelling westwards, to Amlingham and from there we are setting sail to Caldonia. Let us hope the Thundering Sea will keep the demons away." Then the large man looked at Trifan. "You must leave here soon, for they are coming, my boy. The kingdom is doomed; all our worlds will be changed forever." Trifan left the inn quietly, his mood was downbeat, he decided to return to the potting shed and check up on the sword. Back in the peace and tranquillity of the rose gardens, everything appeared a world away from the blacksmith's grim tale. Trifan entered the gloomy confines of the shed, carefully shutting the creaking door behind him, as if not wanting to wake someone asleep.

Everything within the shed had an ageless quality, a place of wonder and secrets. On the bench, lying under the cover of the cloth, lay another secret. Trifan sighed deeply and wished that it would illuminate in a magical glow.

Suddenly, there came a faint knock upon the door. Trifan was so lost in thought, that at first, he didn't notice. The knock was repeated. Quickly, he placed the sword under the bench, hiding it amongst some bags of soil. For a moment he hesitated, wondering who it was.

"Are you going to let me in Trifan? Or do I have to blow the shed down?" boomed a familiar voice from outside.

Trifan's heart leapt as he swiftly released the latch and opened the creaking door into the gloomy garden beyond.

Tumlinfay was standing tall before him, dressed in his dark-green cloak and a wide-brimmed hat. His walking stick was raised in his right hand as if about to knock upon the door.

"Tumlinfay!" exclaimed Trifan with joy. "I wondered if I was ever going to see you again. Why do you call so late?"

Tumlinfay looked down at the boy from under bristling brows. "Are you going to let me in, or do you intend me to be eaten alive by midges?"

"Sorry, please come in; though I guess by your timing it's important?" wondered Trifan.

Once inside the potting shed, Tumlinfay rearranged his hat and sat down upon a large upturned flowerpot, heaving a sigh of relief. "Not getting any younger that's for sure."

"But how did you know I was in here?" asked Trifan, excited but curious about the magician's timing.

"Pure deduction, you see, I know most things. Now then, I think we may need a little light!" The old man then began uttering some strange words.

"Belneth al thonan Rosewene, Mecurial ar ne Eldsmoreth."

Suddenly, a small beam of light emitted from the handle of the crooked walking stick, which steadily grew, until it illuminated the magician and the startled youth, in a large bauble of glimmering light.

"That's better," murmured Tumlinfay. "Eldsmoreth never lets me down."

"Eldsmoreth?" gasped Trifan.

"That's the name of my travelling companion here. He has many magical qualities, as you can see!" Tumlinfay laughed, as he noticed the look of shock on the boy's face.

Trifan looked on aghast, as the walking stick flickered before his eyes. First the sword, now the stick, he wondered if he was going mad.

"Why have you returned tonight?" asked Trifan. "It's not as if I don't want to see you but you are so full of secrets."

"It is an even greater secret that brings me back here tonight, Midsummer's Night," replied Tumlinfay.

Trifan looked up and saw that the magician was pointing the walking stick at him until its tip was an inch from his nose. "Rosewene was asleep but you awakened her. Show me the sword, Trifan, for Eldsmoreth has spoken."

"The sword?" stammered Trifan.

"Yes, the sword," replied Tumlinfay. "Rosewene is her name."

At first, Trifan tensed, thinking the old man had been a fraud and had come to rob him. Then he saw the magician's kind eyes and gentle smile. Trifan reached under the bench and handed the sword over to Tumlinfay. "Are you the owner then? Does it belong to you?" asked the boy. Tumlinfay laughed, as he took the sword in his left hand. The soft light of Eldsmoreth fell upon the sleeping silver of Rosewene.

"No one can own Rosewene," said Tumlinfay, who appeared to be lost in a dream as he stared with fondness at the sword. "She can only be wielded by your hand. She chose you Trifan, to awaken her."

The boy looked on in shock at the sight before him. The light from the stick was covering the sword, almost protecting it.

"I have seen the magic," replied Trifan slowly. "Its light spoke to me, showing a castle with many turrets and a garden with a fair maid dancing." The magician's blue eyes bored into Trifan's soul. Then a faint smile passed his lips. "It is as I thought," he replied. "Rosewene has spoken to you." Still, Tumlinfay gave no secrets away.

After a brief silence, Trifan spoke, his voice low and shaky. "So that's why you were visiting Oakendale, to look for the sword."

"I meant what I said," replied Tumlinfay softly. "I have

always wanted to visit your fayre but somehow never got around to it." Then the old man began to murmur a verse.

"In the shadows of the past, a silver light did shine,
A castle fair of elven-home, Liminulin was its name.
Within its glimmering halls and gardens green,
A sommerling-child was often seen and Rosewene was her name."

"The tale I am about to tell will be beyond your wildest dreams," said Tumlinfay, suddenly flashing his eyes at Trifan. "You are now going to enter a tunnel of darkness that you can either journey with me or back away from. Do you wish me to reveal your destiny, Trifan? Otherwise, I shall leave here with the sword and bother you no more." Tumlinfay's voice trailed away and his gaze dropped to his walking stick.

"I am confused and a little frightened by your words," answered Trifan slowly.

"I would understand if you thought me a little mad," added Tumlinfay.

"A little?" laughed Trifan. "In truth, I have nothing left working here, no family, as such. When you left last time, I wished then that you were taking me on as an apprentice."

Tumlinfay smiled. "I am glad that you trust our friendship, however brief. I am after all getting on a bit. Maybe I could do with a little more of your help." Tumlinfay then handed the sword over to the boy. "You are her guardian now, her keeper. Protect her and she shall protect you. It appears we are entering a dark chapter in Elbion's history. The travellers from the south have many tales to tell. No doubt you have heard them in the taverns. Terror will soon grip the little kingdom, as this new horror creeps nearer. I am afraid your once peaceful life will be a thing of the past." Tumlinfay wiped his brow.

"That is why I am here tonight. Not to warn you but to take you with me."

"But how did you know that I found the sword? Surely you cannot read my mind," Trifan shifted uneasily upon the bench but found that he couldn't escape the light from the sword and stick.

"The night I left here, Eldsmoreth spoke to me," replied Tumlinfay. "He confirmed my suspicions, that these gardens were the resting place of Rosewene and that her magic bathed you."

Trifan scratched his head and looked down at the beautiful sword. He could feel the magician's eyes bore into him as he pondered his future. It felt as if he had wandered, or stumbled, into a dream yet he could feel the cool metal in his palm and the fast beat of his own heart.

After a long silence, Tumlinfay spoke. "The beginning of this dark tale took root many years ago. But even though it had remained buried, deep in the soils of time, the evil has awoken and she has a name."

Tumlinfay rose to his feet and walked to the small window. "Long, long ago, this kingdom was known by another name, one you would not have heard about in the abbey history books. Its name in sommerling verse was Gilindon.

"Before the coming of your ancestors from Caldonia and Albria, Gilindon was a great northern sommerling realm, made up of elves, sprites, pixies and a darker variety of goblin. There are remnants of Gilindon remaining, such as the large stone circles in the west." Tumlinfay turned to face the boy. "As you know from history over a thousand years have passed since the arrival of your forefathers. By then, the land was empty and bereft of life, all sommerlings had vanished."

Trifan frowned. "But how do you know all of this? I thought sommerlings only existed in bedtime stories."

"In time, you will know the answers," replied the magician. "As my new apprentice, you have to trust me. I think you will find me a better employer than this Grimridge fellow! But I will give you answers in time."

"Of course I trust you Tumlinfay and I want you to reveal more." In his palm, the sword began to warm. "Tell me more Mr Tumlinfay about the age of the sommerling."

"The evil that is spreading throughout Elbion has its roots in Gilindon, all those years ago," continued the magician. "It seems that the two ages are mirrored. This time the land cannot be overrun by darkness as Gilindon was all those years ago."

Tumlinfay paused to wipe his brow. "That is why I am

here tonight, to unveil your true destiny, dangerous as it is."

The light from Eldsmoreth lit up the magician's sharp features and furrowed brow. Tumlinfay appeared to Trifan as if he belonged to another world. Maybe Tumlinfay was of sommerling blood.

8

Tumlinfay Unveils
the Past

AFTER a long silence, Tumlinfay spoke. "If I hadn't
discovered my travelling friend here," he said,
looking fondly at the gnarled stick. "Then I would have no
part to play in this strange tale. Whether it was by chance
that I found him, or destiny, I don't have the answer. Was
it fate, Master Foxley, that guided your hand upon Rosewene after all those years, who can say?"

The magician loosened his heavy cloak and fixed his
eyes upon the boy.

"I can see that you are still unsure about me and who
can blame you, so I shall tell you my own tale."

The boy sat in silence, entranced by the magician's
hypnotic words, words that at first would wash over him,
then rear up and shake him to the marrow. "My real name
is Tum, just plain Tum," continued the magician. "Tumlinfay means, quite simply, Tum-of-the magic, a name I
inherited after university. I was a little older than you

when I first discovered Eldsmoreth and was studying at the great Garfax University. I was always a curious fellow, rather like you and it was my curiosity that changed my life. It began one winter's morning in the year 1020 when I first observed the strange movements of a prefect, a promising sorcerer, called Proudsickle. It was from the window of my lodgings that I saw him lead the Grandmaster's prized horse, Bria, from the stables and ride out through the east gate. He repeated this strange routine the same time every morning, for days, until one night, he returned on foot, without the horse.

"For many months, I would watch as Proudsickle would lead another mount from the stable yard and ride out along the winding lane away from Garfax and its many turrets. The mysterious disappearance of Bria was now old news, though the previous February rumours had seized Garfax of a giant wolf that would scale the high walls and drag the unfortunate beast to its death, devoured in the countryside beyond.

"But as the months wore on and the Grandmaster's anger subsided, the disappearance was soon forgotten and as was the custom of the University, students would never tell tales. Proudsickle's bizarre actions were to remain a secret, except from me.

"By the following summer, in the year 1021, I decided to miss my afternoon lesson and follow the prefect. Because of Proudsickle's new power and stature within Garfax, he was never questioned and never approached. But his long absences and strange movements were noted. Most put it down to a restless spirit, or a high intellect, linked to eccentricity or even madness. I was on edge. Many times I wished I had slept on that distant summer's morning. Now of course, my curiosity had been aroused and as an inquisitive eighteen-year-old, that spelt trouble.

"Whenever I crossed Proudsickle's path, whether in the map-room or the peaceful herb gardens, we would exchange a knowing look, with the prefect flashing me a sly smile. But it was his penetrating eyes that would always chill my bones. On midsummer's day, as the sun was at its strongest, I saw Proudsickle make his move. Leading out another mount from the stables, I observed him pass under the east archway and clatter away along the lane. Untethering a friendly but rather slow mare called Meredith I too passed under the arch but kept to the willow-lined bank, to the side of the cobbled lane.

"Although I kept out of sight, I knew Proudsickle would sense my presence. It was said that when he sniffed the air, he was smelling his way around, using his nose as a third eye. I did tremble at that thought and reined in Meredith. As I sat in the saddle, I could hear the tapping of hooves gradually getting fainter, as the prefect carried on his familiar passage to Tangleroot Forest. My curiosity was too much to bear.

"Something though began to agitate Meredith. I ran my fingers through her thick mane and whispered words of encouragement. "Do not worry my friend, you will not be journeying under Tangleroot's eaves today," Meredith shook her head as she understood my kind words, for she knew that none of her friends had returned from the trees.

"Whatever black-beard is up to, will have to wait."

"I wiped my brow free from beads of sweat and gazed around at the rich, green countryside that now lay baking under a relentless June sun."

"All was quiet and still, it was almost as if the very wind had been sucked from the sky."

"From the corner of my eye, I noticed a lone, white butterfly dancing along the top of the hedgerow. I watched it rest on the hawthorn and then take to the air once more. It made me think. I had travelled six miles from Garfax, was only a mile from the fringes of Tangleroot Forest, yet I felt I was standing at the gates of another world. Maybe it was the heat or the eerie stillness, but something had awoken my sixth sense."

"Suddenly, Meredith began to kick and lurch and in a swift motion, unbecoming of a stocky workhorse, reared up, sending me crashing into the deep ditch by the side of the road. While I groaned and rolled in the nettles and cow parsley, Meredith simply wandered over the cobbles and began grazing on the tempting grass beyond."

"When I opened my eyes, I found myself sprawled upon a bed of crushed nettles. I scrambled to my feet and could see Meredith chewing contentedly upon the abundant grass under a clear blue sky. It was then that I saw it for the first time, poking out from an abandoned rabbit hole. I fell to my knees and dug out the earth that clung to its form. It was too straight to be a tree root and at its tip had strange letters carved deep into the wood. Finally, I wrenched it free from its resting place with such force, that I fell backwards into the bed of nettles." He laughed at the memory.

"The walking stick, though gnarled, was beautiful to behold. For a breathless moment, I just stared at its form, something, I knew not, what was beginning to seduce me, as though an unseen light was wrapping its warm form around my body, protecting me. Then the moment passed. 'You really are just an old, carved walking stick,' I muttered to myself. I ran my fingers in and out of the deep runes that ran the length of its twisted body. I wondered what the words meant and why somebody would bother with such intricate carvings. My first inkling was to show the strange stick to my best friend, Sirifix, but then as I gazed down upon its form I decided it was best to keep it safe and keep it secret."

Trifan watched as the old man gripped the stick ever more tightly.

"I found the stick useful in many ways," he continued, "For I enjoyed rambling through woods and fields and the dear old stick never left my side, it was my constant companion. The years of study passed swiftly and soon I turned from apprentice to teacher and my beard from grey to white. But my world turned upside down fifty, or so, years later. It was one stormy night back in February, at home in my library in Golenwood, that the most incredible scene began to unfold. I was working late upon some manuscripts, when suddenly, my beloved walking stick, which was resting upon the dining table, began to glow in the most eerie light. To my utmost horror and then amazement, a voice started to flow. The voice coming from the walking-stick was Elvish."

Tumlinfay gazed fondly at his stick. "It is a language of sommerling that I had been familiar with at Garfax. I just sat there and listened, enchanted by this magic before me. In a whispered voice, he told me that his name was Eldsmoreth, that he was once a knight of Gilindon. He spoke of his undying love for the King's daughter and that he had rescued her from death. He spoke clearly, yet with sorrow. He wanted to know what form he now took and where he had lain for the past thousand years. When I said he had taken the form of a walking stick, I was sure I could hear the soft sound of weeping, coming from the wood."

Tumlinfay dabbed his eye with a handkerchief. "In under an hour, Eldsmoreth had told me a history of Gilindon, of the vanishing of the sommerlings and the emergence of mortals. He also said he had awoken to warn me and for me to find his beloved, an elf princess called Rosewene, before Morgalene is awoken from her slumber. Fate, my boy, has connected us all." Trifan sat open-mouthed as the words registered. He had been chosen to awake her and he had held her in his own mortal hands. He felt ashamed at how grubby they had been.

"Eldsmoreth then told me of the task that I had to undertake," continued the magician, "That, my dear Trifan, is how I became involved. This was his tale:

"Long ago, in the age of sommerling, there ruled a great king. His name was Barunion, protector of Gilindon and her four seas. He was a wise ruler, stout of heart, yet kind and thoughtful in nature. The story of his demise came with the death of his beloved wife, Queen Iwilder. To cure his broken heart, he took to fighting overseas in the Unicorn wars. But he was struck down by an arrow and doomed never to see his beloved Gilindon again. To Liminulin castle, they bore his lifeless body across a dark, silent land, lit only by the pyres that burned and flickered upon every hill." Tumlinfay then began to chant a verse.

> "Over thundering seas, the king returned,
> To a winter's land murk and cold,
> Whereupon every hill a pyre did burn, in memory of their
> lord so bold.
> Across the realm his body they bore, To Liminulin's gate and
> castle door.
> With sorrowed hearts the sommerlings weep,
> As for all eternity, their king shall sleep."

"The Elvish words are somehow lost with our own guttural tongue." Tumlinfay blew his nose on a handkerchief. "The cause of all our problems lay with what followed and King Barunion's final decree.

"As his body was carried to the castle, his two young daughters, overcome with grief and sorrow, threw themselves upon their beloved father. They were princesses whom the sommerlings called 'night and day'. Rosewene had hair as fine as spun gold while Morgalene had locks as black as pitch, with a streak of silver running from her crown. For this she was teased, for grey was an unlucky symbol amongst the sommerlings, many thought she was cursed. In reality, she was."

Tumlinfay's words flowed into Trifan's mind as this new world opened up to him. The air inside the potting shed became stuffy, yet the boy was not crouching amongst the bags of soil and the many cobwebs but transported to Gilindon where he was looking down upon a castle of white, with many banners fluttering from its lofty towers.

Tumlinfay cleared his throat and continued. "As they mourned, the successor to the throne was announced. The air tingled with disbelief and for a moment, time stood still. Barunion had named his youngest daughter, Rosewene, to be crowned upon his death. Morgalene, who was ten years older, was thought to be a creature of ill-omen. At this news, she did indeed bring misfortune, as Eldsmoreth was witness, to the terrible scene that unfolded, as Morgalene screamed in anger and fled from the hall in a rage. "How can she be queen!" she hissed, her once delicate features turning to cold stone. "I am the elder, it should be me, not my snivelling little sister." In a corner of

Morgalene's mind, where once she had known laughter and sunlight, terrible darkness grew.

"Waiting for the princess within her chamber, was Dragool, her personal sorcerer, a most loathsome creature of goblin blood.

"Do not despair!" he rasped, stepping forth from the shadows. "You shall still be queen and I, your most loyal servant. My magic can serve you well, let you drink from the cup of youth."

"Morgalene looked at the white-bearded, half goblin, fixing him with her black eyes. "Speak!"

"You shall remain beautiful forever, while your sister of gold shall fade and die," he continued, "And when she is dead, you will rule Gilindon." He smiled up at her, revealing a set of razor-sharp teeth.

"Tell me more, Dragool," she replied coldly, "And your rewards will surely follow."

"Together, Morgalene and her sorcerer plotted their evil dreams. With her reputation for ill-omen and a new streak of cruelty, the sommerlings at court gave her a wide berth. The following winter, on her orders, Morgalene's followers raided the royal stables and slaughtered Rosewene's prized unicorns, once captured by her father during the previous year's war. It was said that Morgalene and Dragool feasted on their flesh and drank their sacred blood."

Tumlinfay wiped his brow. Trifan, who sat quite still, noticed how much the magician sweated. It was almost as if he had been present in those dreadful times and had witnessed those terrible sights.

"Though nothing was proved, the suspicion fell on Morgalene," said the magician, "While Rosewene, sensing that her sister had brought a shadow to the realm, banished her to the distant grim castle of Grizilder. The castle still lies deep in your shire of Mortenden. For many years, Rosewene ruled Gilindon with kindness and grace; the land grew fat, green and free of war and famine. She was known as the elf-of-the-rose, as she spent every moonlit evening, singing and dancing in the gardens of Liminulin. That, my boy, was the vision you witnessed."

Tumlinfay rose to his feet and walked to the small window, where he stooped to gaze out. "As the years passed, Morgalene and Dragool continued to practise their growing magic, deep within the dark forgotten vaults of Grizilder and many sommerlings of evil intent flocked to her banner. Every night in her loftiest tower, Morgalene, draped in her cloak of bat fur would gaze into a mirror of framed serpents. In her hand, she would drink fresh blood and admire her fine, ageless face. Her raven-black hair grew so long, while the silver streak was dyed red." Tumlinfay turned at looked at Trifan, who sat quite still. "But it was one long winter's night, twenty years after King Barunion's death, that a macabre scene unfolded. Once more Morgalene gazed into her mirror. The serpents hissed and licked with approval upon seeing their queen. Slowly, she caressed her skin and stroked her long hair.

"Soon I shall be the queen of all Gilindon." But her voice was not youthful, yet croaked and harsh. When she looked deep into the mirror, she saw her face had aged and withered into the mask of a monster. Oh, how she screamed, "Dragool, your craft is failing me!" She had the face of a creature two-hundred years old."

Tumlinfay paused for breath. "Morgalene's desire for more fresh blood grew, so much so, that soon travellers began to mysteriously vanish if they ventured too near Grizilder. Rumours spread throughout the land of sommerling-ghouls, werewolves and blood-drinking demons. Every village in the west became deserted."

The magician sat back down upon the flowerpot. The silence in the shed was stifling. "Rosewene was so alarmed at the news that had been brought back by her scouts, she assembled an army and so marched upon Grizilder. What she found within the mountains of Undain was a vast army of ghouls waiting for her, with Morgalene, a sister she had once loved above all else, riding at the helm, upon a chariot, decorated with the skulls of her victims." In the garden beyond, the sudden hoot of an owl made Trifan jump. "Beneath Grizilder's shadow a dreadful battle was fought," continued Tumlinfay, "The first of the Sommerling- Wars. Upon the battlefield, all was lost. Rosewene's army was ill-prepared and ill-equipped. Their years of prosperity made them weak. Her army was cut down or imprisoned, more fresh blood for Morgalene, no doubt. Her desire for the throne was quenched, like her thirst for blood. In the dungeons of Grizilder, a silver sword was crafted. This was to be Rosewene's fate, imprisonment within the sword, a prison contrived by Dragool. I am sure his reward followed." Tumlinfay then kissed the tip of the walking stick. "Only one elf remained. Eldsmoreth was a young knight of Gilindon, tall and fair. Across the battle-field he rode, passing under Grizilder's mighty shadow. He was Rosewene's guardian, her one true love.

"Eldsmoreth never unveiled his journey into Grizilder with me, he would only tell of his fear and horror. He remembered cutting down Rosewene as she hung like an ornament above Morgalene's throne of skulls. Then he fled for his life, with the sword at his side. He mounted his steed and made the perilous journey over the mountains of Undain, hearing only the cry of fell-creatures and wolves above the fearsome winds. Then he escaped north-wards, through a land bereft of life, decorated only with fields of burning stubble. In his account, he mentioned clearly the vast forest to the west, which would be Lineer and then crossing a great river, which would be the broad River Wand, in Fallowden."

Trifan sat entranced, he had studied all the maps of Elbion thoroughly and he could follow Eldsmoreth's escape in his mind.

"He mentions passing between forest and rounded hill," continued Tumlinfay relentlessly, "Which I take as being the eastern tip of Whitewebbs and the rolling East Downs and then over the fertile lands of Fluxen, with its many orchards. He nearly drowned crossing the River Buck and witnessed the army of ghouls gathering on the bank behind. Amongst the ranks of goblin-sommerlings, he could see the lofty form of Morgalene, standing tall in her chariot. He pressed wearily on, until soon he was at the gates of Liminulin, now deserted. He rushed to the secret rose gardens where he buried her deep within the sacred soil, under the shade of a magnolia tree. After fleeing Liminulin, Eldsmoreth, now racked with pain and hunger, was eventually captured in the south of Camelon. There he was spared death, surprisingly, but turned into a crooked walking-stick, a mockery of his standing, to endure an everlasting prison of torment. Then he was tossed into a ditch."

Trifan gazed in awe at the weathered stick, yet saw no signs of life. A flicker of doubt crossed his mind.

"It was fate that I found Eldsmoreth that summer day, just as fate guided your hand upon Rosewene," said the magician softly. "We were both chosen for this immense task. After this most spectacular tale, Eldsmoreth told me of the quest I had to undertake and the reason he had awoken from his sleep. He said I had to search for Rosewene, to seek out the garden of Liminulin, which lay upon the willow-banks of the river Maluin. This is how he spoke in rhyme to me.

"Seek out my queen, oh dear and trusty friend,
Search far and wide, until journey end,

Look out for Liminulin and a garden of red rose and green,
Growing by the bank of the Maluin. Look under the roots of a
* magnolia tree,*
And there you shall find my dancing queen."

"I would sit through the many long hours of conversation entranced by his elf-tongue, so different from my sommerling lessons at university. It took me many nights poring over sommerling manuscripts, ones that had been rescued from the great fire at Garfax. I soon discovered that a King Barunion had lived, had indeed fought in the Unicorn wars and had two daughters, Rosewene and Morgalene."

"What happened to Morgalene, Mr Tumlinfay, did she die?" asked Trifan curiously.

"How her empire crumbled, I do not know," replied the magician. "When your ancestors arrived in their long-boats from Caldonia and Albria, it was recorded by the monks that all they found was an island bereft of life, with only the relics of cairns and lonely standing stones. The race of sommerling had departed. In answer to your last point, alas, Morgalene is alive once more and even now is stalking the grim vaults of Grizilder."

Trifan gasped and put a hand to his mouth.

"Eldsmoreth though would only talk in riddles. He would ramble incoherently, other days he would talk only of his broken heart and of his lonely years, locked within the confines of his wooden prison. All in all, it took the whole month of February and most of March, before the tale was told in full." Tumlinfay sighed heavily.

"But, how could you be certain the tale was true, that you were not going mad?" asked Trifan. "Perhaps the stick was bewitched."

"I know you still think of me as eccentric," smiled Tumlinfay. "But I found my new predicament too strange to comprehend. But such was my fifty-year association with this most delightful of walking sticks, I simply believed his words. My task was to find the location of Liminulin and there I would find the keeper of Rosewene. I had to find you by midsummer at least, or else it would be too late."

Tumlinfay raised himself from his seat and clambered over to the window once more. He brushed aside a cobweb and gazed out, almost as if he were expecting somebody. Trifan shifted uneasily. "I eventually discovered that your pretty market town of Oakendale matched the very site of Liminulin. I knew that in May, there was a famous Rose Fayre. So, I made up my mind and began to make the necessary preparations to fly north, in my new flying contraption and so seek out the keeper of the gardens; you."

9

The Willing Apprentice

TRIFAN remained absolutely silent and gazed down at the magic sword that lay in his palm. He looked up and saw Tumlinfay's blue eyes, sparkling back at him in the gloom. The light from Eldsmoreth had faded, as all around the darkness closed in.

"Soon Morgalene and her host will be on the move again, as it was in Eldsmoreth's time," said the magician. "From her fastness of Grizilder, she will lay waste to the soft lands, slaying all in her path. This time her thirst for blood must be unquenchable. By some dark magic, she knows that Eldsmoreth has awoken and Rosewene discovered. For she is not only drawn to her sister, but she will also be drawn to whoever holds her."

"But, how did Morgalene awake after all these years?" asked Trifan quietly. "Her very name chills me to the bone."

"I do not know," replied Tumlinfay. "I fear there is great mischievousness at work, dead witches do not suddenly awake. I fear someone has breathed life into her."

"How long do we have until she comes here?" Trifan had a dull ache in the pit of his stomach, after the elation of seeing the magician once more, he now felt confused and in shock. "Is that why you disappeared so quickly after the Rose Fayre?"

Tumlinfay looked at the boy in surprise. "You are a perceptive young man. I think Rosewene has chosen well.

"After my departure from Oakendale, I knew that Rosewene had been discovered and that she was in safe hands. Eldsmoreth was pleased with you. He said you were the one."

Trifan felt a sudden surge of pride. He looked at the old, gnarled walking stick, wondering if it would speak to him there and then. Instead, it just glimmered in its faint, yellow light.

"Eldsmoreth said that we were safe until after midsummer. So with over a month to find more answers, I decided to leave your side and take a closer look at Mortenden. After dropping in at home, I collected some provisions and with a dear friend of mine, Sirifix, flew my contraption south."

"What did you see?" asked Trifan.

"Alas, Eldsmoreth's prophecy had taken hold. All the lands south of the River Wand are now deserted, bereft of life in cottage, farmstead and village. Fear has spread like fire on straw."

Trifan swallowed hard and gripped the sword tightly. Elbion, had always been safe and secure, a place where misery and suffering belonged to the past. He looked up and met Tumlinfay's sharp gaze.

"Under the cold face of a full moon, we floated over the high crags of Undain, a place of dread, even you have heard. We saw for ourselves a desolate land of marsh and forests of thorn. But it was the spectacle of Grizilder, rising like a claw, from the very centre of that grim land that appalled us the most." Tumlinfay shook his head. "Grizilder is very much alive, my boy; fires were lit below and there was movement on the ground." Trifan sat caked in sweat, his mouth opens wide. He remembered the blacksmith's tale at the inn. Maybe it was time to leave these shores, to sail abroad.

"In time Morgalene would follow you to other lands," said the magician reading his thoughts. "There is no escape."

"But this is terrible, what am I to do?" stammered Trifan.

"For the moment, nothing and secondly, I would like it if you left here tonight with me," replied the magician solemnly. His eyes darted to the door. "I can sense danger is nearer than we think. We cannot hide, Trifan. Both the sword and walking stick have bathed our bodies in magic. We are now Morgalene's desire. She already has eyes on these beautiful rose gardens." Trifan suddenly jumped to his feet, gripping Rosewene by the hilt. "I thought I heard something."

"Be still," urged Tumlinfay. "You will need to handle

Rosewene once we venture towards Grizilder. For that is our path, only you can slay Morgalene and so save the little kingdom from the second age of terror."

Tumlinfay knew he had said too much to the boy, too soon. He should have waited until they had reached the safety of Golenwood. He watched Trifan anxiously for his response. The keeper had to come willingly. He hoped the boy would trust him.

Trifan had sat back down again. His pale eyes shone out from behind a youthful thatch of fair hair.

"We must leave tonight," said Tumlinfay, "For it is nearly midnight on midsummer's eve. If you decide to remain, then that is your choice. But I returned tonight for Rosewene, whether or not, you accept your destiny as her keeper. I am sorry it had to be you." Trifan looked up unsmiling.

"At least I can keep an eye on you if you come with me," assured Tumlinfay with a smile. "You are after all my willing apprentice."

After a long silence, Trifan spoke. "I feel as though I need a new path to follow. Oakendale holds nothing for me now. I shall willingly come with you, though I have never wielded a sword before."

"Though Mortenden is a long way off yet, we have no time to lose," said the magician, relieved at the boy's decision. He knew that if he had remained, he would have been slayed before the night was up. He had to get him to

Golenwood. "We have to leave now. I am sorry there is no time for fond farewells, not even for your friends."

"But where do we go tonight?" asked Trifan. He wondered what his friends, or, even the grumbling Grimridge would make of his sudden disappearance. He knew that he wouldn't be welcome upon his return. If, of course, he did return. That thought bothered him.

"Come, Trifan," reassured the magician, "It is time to go."

Together, they left the potting shed. Trifan glanced back for the final time, then the door creaked shut. He had left his world behind. His heart sank. "Let us look once more upon the enchantment of Liminulin," sighed Tumlinfay. "You have tended your gardens well."

The magician stood silent, smiling contentedly and breathing in the flowering scents. Then in a low voice he began to chant.

"In Liminulin's secret garden,
On midsummer's night,
They shall all gather,
The Sommerling Queen, the Keeper
And Eldsmoreth still shining bright."

Trifan suddenly felt uneasy, as though they were being spied upon. He could sense unfriendly eyes watching him with resentment and anger. He peered into the gloom, yet Tumlinfay remained motionless. "I think we are being watched," whispered Trifan.

"We are!" snapped Tumlinfay. "Quick, let us make haste to the meadow." The magician turned swiftly and strode off through the dark gardens, towards the northern gates. The night air was chill as he stumbled clumsily behind Tumlinfay. This was not the adventure he had in mind.

Before Trifan had time to think, he had passed under the ivy-clad archway of the north gates. He suddenly stopped and looked back. He could see the shadowy outline of the small trees and rosebushes, outlined beyond, his home and life for many happy years. Just then, a tawny owl screeched above his head, making him jump.

"Hurry my lad," called out Tumlinfay. "You shall return to your roses one day, I promise. For now, your new life awaits you!"

Together they crossed a silent and deserted Barnyard's Lane, over the swift-flowing River Freshbright and on past the solemn shape of the old church. The shadows had lengthened into blackness, though a house opposite the church still had the light of a candle in the upper window. Trifan's unease grew steadily worse. It felt as if he was leaving his past and journeying through a portal, a dark tunnel, to another more terrifying world. He hoped he was right about the mysterious Mr Tumlinfay.

They climbed the wide stile at the side of the church wall and dropped down into the long fragrant grass of the meadow. High above, a strip of cloud uncovered a full moon and in the black canvas of a night sky, a billion specks of starlight jostled for attention.

Then he saw Tumlinfay's contraption, hovering in the centre of the meadow, spewing flames like a fat, bloated dragon. The basket, which was only a few feet from the ground, was held in place with four support ropes, while standing within the basket, Trifan could see a plumper and shorter version of Tumlinfay. This figure was waving his arms at them as they approached, though not in greeting but a warning. "Tumlinfay we are not alone, they are here, in the meadow!" he cried. "What took you so long?" He held out a chubby hand to Trifan. "I am Sirifix by the way, come on lad, I'll haul you up." For a moment Sirifix paused, as he noticed the sword. Then Tumlinfay's voice shook him free from his temporary trance.

"Are you sure?" The magician turned to face the open gloom of the meadow. He sniffed the air and then gazed up at the stars. "What have you seen?"

"I heard a hideous howl," gasped Sirifix, "Over by the far hedge. While you were sniffing roses, I was listening to blood-curdling cries!"

Suddenly, as Tumlinfay was about to climb into the basket, they heard the most dreadful, haunting cry. The long-drawn-out wail was sure to wake the townsfolk. "Morgalene's servants are here!" cried the magician.

Then another hideous howl greeted the first then a third joined in, as did a fourth, fifth and then sixth. Trifan covered his ears in terror. Sirifix took Eldsmoreth, while Tumlinfay climbed into the rocking basket.

Sirifix then took out a small knife and began to sever the ropes, one by one.

Then they appeared, six ghostly, white shapes, moving swiftly from the far hedge. A thin mist rose from the grass, adding to this ethereal, yet terrifying vision.

Sirifix sliced the first rope, sending the basket off balance and Tumlinfay off his feet. The flames from the dragon spat and hissed as if in a warning. Sirifix cut the second rope, still, the ghastly shapes which appeared to be floating upon the swirling mists, came into view. Trifan gasped in horror, they had sounded wolf-like but they were enormous creatures, twice the size and gruesome to the point of deformity.

The giant balloon, suddenly swung to one side, knocking Trifan to his knees and his sword clattering out of his grasp.

Tumlinfay sliced the third rope, sending the orb into the opposite direction. What came from the shadows, clinging to their tendrils of mist, would haunt Trifan for years to come. Their snouts were long, while fixed either side, protruding upwards like a pair of curved daggers, were two giant teeth. Terror seized them. Sirifix dropped his small knife, while the basket swung like a pendulum, across the long grass. "The ghouls are here!" he cried. "The ghouls are here!"

The leading creature leapt into the air and clawed its way upon the side of the basket, its terrible jaws wide open and demonic, red eyes burning brightly.

Tumlinfay struggled with the last support rope but then a second creature, leapt upon the other side of the basket; Trifan turned and found himself staring into the face of a monster. He staggered back, grasped Rosewene frantically and swung the glinting blade down upon the grotesque, thick neck of the creature, which had begun to crawl its way into the basket. As the sword fell, the ghoul exploded into a mushroom of white dust, which dropped to the ground below. Tumlinfay thrust his own knife into the red socket of the other ghoul which too exploded loudly, its deathly scream fading with the falling dust.

With a final slice from Rosewene, the last support rope was severed and with a sudden, heavy jolt, Tumlinfay's contraption, began to float effortlessly upward, into the deepness of the night. From the mist-shrouded meadow below, illuminated only by a single shaft of moonbeam, they could see the remaining four ghouls, howling and gnashing in a frenzy and then, as if they too were struck by a magical sword, suddenly explode in a crackle and final scream of disintegrating white dust.

Tumlinfay, in all his long life, had never seen anything so horrific. He turned to look at his new apprentice, who was slumped on the floor, gripping the sword and shaking with shock. The boy had learned quickly.

Trifan looked over and saw the magician smiling at him. He couldn't believe his dream was coming true. He was leaving Oakendale with Tumlinfay, heading into new lands for adventure, though not the sort would have dreamt about in a million years.

"Steer a wind's course to Golenwood, my dear Sirifix," said Tumlinfay. "South to the west and south again."

From the consuming gloom, far below, a pair of eyes agonized over their escape. Proudsickle gripped the ugly box, ever tighter. He had been a veritable fool; he had left it too late. "I shall be better prepared at Golenwood, my apprentice Tum. Then I will be leaving with the sword and the walking stick. You will not survive the next of Morgalene's gifts." As the clouds covered the moon, so a shadow covered his heart. He knew one of Morgalene's gifts had been squandered. He wondered if she would be so forgiving. He pulled his long dark hood over his head and slipped from the meadow to his awaiting horse that had been tethered in the lane. The animal shifted uneasily, as its master approached with the box. It could sense the presence of evil.

Proudsickle opened a large leather pouch at the horse's side but the animal suddenly reared up in terror, frothing at the mouth. "Come, come, Askalon, I will never harm you," he whispered soothingly. "You are my favourite, you do know that. The box is a gift from our most wonderous Queen." The horse settled and Proudsickle swung skilfully onto the saddle. It was to be a long and fruitless journey back to Grendeline. He could hear Morgalene inside his head already but tonight he wouldn't answer. Not tonight. After this failure, he knew that loathsome Grib would take advantage. The foul sprite's task was to invade the Sommerlands, with his own box of gifts, a much trickier affair though. Deep down Proudsickle wished him dead. The sorcerer stroked Askalon's neck. The horse's body was caked in sweat, even though the late air was chill. His mind moved from his old sommerling acquaintance to his one-time friend, now rival. "You are a strange being, Tumlinfay. There is something about you, some greater mystery. You are worth capturing, not killing. Your escape was good, though."

Askalon shifted uneasily, he knew his master was mad.

"Then we shall meet again, on Mistletoe Eve, my dear Tum."

Proudsickle turned his horse into the east road and vanished from view.

10

Golenwood

TRIFAN drifted in and out of sleep. Despite the horrors he had witnessed he continued to slumber peacefully.

When he awoke, he could feel the chill air stroke his face and the rhythmic bellowing breath of the dragon, as the basket gently swayed, making him feel at peace.

When he next opened his eyes, the swirling tendrils of cloud had disappeared, yet as he stirred, he could see soft lights far below, lights in a myriad of glimmering colours.

"Brace yourselves!" cried Sirifix, in a voice that shook Trifan's senses. As he gazed curiously below, he could see long rows of lights, flickering orbs of green, blue, gold and white, filing away from the broad silver strip of a river up to a long low house of thatch that itself sat within a protective cluster of trees and a mature garden.

Beyond that comforting sight, he could see an impenetrable dark mass, covering, it seemed, all the lands to the south.

Trifan wondered if they had flown to the dark open seas or the very end of the world.

"This is my beloved Golenwood," said Tumlinfay with a reassuring hand on the boy's shoulder. "While beyond is the vast green realm of Whitewebbs."

"Hold on tight!" exclaimed Sirifix.

Trifan's heart dropped into his mouth as the basket first descended sharply, then lurched to the right as it skimmed the river, flooding the basket with water.

"Kissing the River Swanflight!" laughed Sirifix.

The basket then lurched forward unto the bank digging up great tufts of grass. "Mind the lawn!" scolded Tumlinfay.

Trifan tried hard not to laugh but before he could cry out was sent flying to his knees, as they came to a sudden halt.

The dragon wheezed a final strain of breath before the bulk of canvas deflated and then collapsed over them.

"Welcome to Golenwood!" came the voice of Sirifix from somewhere within the folds of canvas. "Hope you had a pleasant flight".

As Trifan climbed free from the basket, he looked around in wonder. It was the most enchanting house he had ever seen. He walked over to the light and placed his fingers upon its glimmering red form. The orb was set upon a long iron pole.

"They are powered by the sun and made from expensive Amlingham glass", said Tumlinfay, as he proceeded the slow job of folding up the vast canvas into the basket.

About eighty such lights were lining either side of that broad sweep of lawn, each nestling under a small scented fruit tree. The lights and trees led up to a winding pebbled path that climbed up through a rock garden of ferns and small pools of water until finally it ended at the foot of Golenwood. "An ancient house", added Sirifix, who was now breathing heavily, as both magicians struggled up the lawn with the basket. "It was built in the reign of Queen Ellawene."

"Why was it built here, so near the forest?" asked Trifan.

"The owner built it by the forest because that was where he had last seen his sommerling-bride," replied Tumlinfay. "He thought she would return to him one day."

Trifan looked up at the old magician, who in turn smiled down at him. "Come," said Tumlinfay, "Let's go inside and have supper."

Sirifix and the magician carried the basket, contents and all, up to the inviting house. At the end of the lawn, there flowed a small stream that was straddled by a footbridge. On the other side, a narrow path of purple slate wound gradually upwards, between thick beds of shrubs and hollyhocks; for a fleeting moment, Trifan longed for his home, his rose gardens. Then he saw Golenwood and a strange feeling of love and warmth washed over him. The old house was enchanting beyond belief, yet though its creaking timbers and thick hair of thatch lent it a vulnerable look, Trifan looked up in awe, sensing some powerful force of good.

"I was the same as you when I first set eyes on her," said Tumlinfay. "She can even help cure a broken heart."

Before Trifan could ask what he meant, the magician spoke again. "We shall of course be safe enough here."

"Can we leave this lot on the porch tonight?" panted Sirifix. "I am getting far too old for this." Trifan laughed aloud.

"Of course," replied Tumlinfay. "May I remind you, dear Sirifix, I also happen to be a lot older than you."

Once across the threshold of Golenwood, Trifan felt the horror at the meadow ease away. The house not only appeared warm and snug but felt as though he was standing within an ancient, secret abode that was now aware of his presence.

It was as if each stone, each thick beam and knotted floorboard, tingled and flowed with a life of its own.

As Trifan gazed around the magician's cottage, he noticed, to his surprise, that it contained none of the usual paraphernalia or magical accessories. There were no crystal-balls, no strange maps, no scurrying animals and no bubbling potions; just luxurious rugs and expensive foreign tapestries, a shining silver coat of armour in the hall, even a magnificent grandfather clock that chimed in the most beautiful way.

Before the boy could ask where his magic tricks were

kept, Tumlinfay was striding down the long hallway and proceeded to light the many suspended oil lamps as he went. "Welcome to Golenwood, my home for the last fifty years," he called out. As soon as he had lit the final lamp a look of tired pleasure crossed his face. "Much better, can't use up all of Eldsmoreth's light tonight, can we?"

MAP OF GOLENWOOD

That first night, Trifan soon forgot about the ghouls in the meadow. Soon he was feasting on a meal of rabbit stew and apple pie.

Tumlinfay, who sat opposite, watched him closely while drinking tea from a large green pot.

As Sirifix climbed the stairs to bed, so Tumlinfay showed the weary boy to his bedroom. In an instant, Trifan fell asleep, with Rosewene by his side. The magician sat at his bedside for a while, with Eldsmoreth upon his lap. Then the old man began to sing a short verse as the yellowing light from the lamp flickered.

> *"When greensward leaves begin to wither and the snows*
> *begin to fall.*
> *Fear, not the creeping darkness,*
> *For the Prince of the Sommerlings shall hear our call."*

When Trifan awoke the following morning, he found Tumlinfay snoring loudly on the leather chair in the corner of the room. The magician suddenly snorted, coughed and propped himself up with the aid of the strange walking stick. "Ah, good morning young man, I trust you had a restful sleep. Golenwood never disappoints."

That morning, after breakfast, Tumlinfay led Trifan into a small room that looked out east into the scented herb garden. The morning's sunlight lit up a cluttered world of old books and manuscripts, most of which were stacked in high shelves, or scattered upon the floor. It reminded Trifan of the map room at Oakendale Abbey.

"My library," said Tumlinfay proudly. "This is where most of my work has taken place over the years. This is, perhaps, the greatest library of sorcery left in the kingdom, especially now as the once magnificent Garfax University has gone."

"What happened to it?" asked Trifan curiously.

"In the year 1035, it mysteriously caught fire and was turned to ash," replied the magician sadly. "Some say it was deliberate, though we were always experimenting with sulphur and flame. Ironically, it started in Proudsickle's own lodgings. He was my old tutor and now, of course, is head of our Order. You shall meet him soon on Mistletoe Eve, when all my old friends from Garfax will attend a Gathering."

Trifan picked up the nearest book which was covered in a fine layer of dust and then blew upon the cover.

"Healing with herbs and mosses," said the boy. "Does it really work?"

Tumlinfay smiled. "Well, I haven't caught a cold in fifty years," replied the magician, who then began to cough as the rising dust tickled his nose. Trifan laughed and then coughed himself.

"Sorcery is only an extension of healing and cures. These cures are growing all around us, in the woods, fields and especially the hedgerows; a veritable apothecary of potions."

As the magician spoke, Trifan glanced out of the small window that looked out over a vibrant herb garden of sage, parsley and mint, where the tall red tips of 'hotlips', acted as a beacon for the many bees. Beyond the tidy garden were the first outer branches of an ancient forest of oaks, with twisted arms and gnarled trunks.

Tumlinfay followed the boy's gaze.

"That is Whitewebbs, the largest forest in Elbion. You could walk from my garden to the East Downs of Fallowden and never leave the shadows of the trees; most terrifying, yet most remarkable."

"Whitewebbs!" exclaimed Trifan. "I have heard about the legends." His friend Tervy had once ventured to Lynd on its borders to stay with an uncle.

"You could lose yourself within shouting distance of Golenwood," replied Tumlinfay. "Who knows what secrets lie hidden. I have only walked a mile into her domain, collecting firewood, or picking mushrooms.

Even then I can hear the trees whispering amongst themselves. Most incredible."

"For one so wise, I didn't think you would believe in superstitions," added Trifan with surprise.

"When you live so near to something so ancient, you have to respect its secrets."

"Can we have a closer look?" pressed the boy. "After all the sun is shining."

Tumlinfay smiled and beckoned Trifan to follow him. He led the boy out of a side door that opened upon a narrow cobbled path, which in turn filed away through the swaying patches of herbs and eventually out to a small meadow that sloped upward to a low hedge, over which hung the first outer branches of the forest. Tumlinfay walked with Trifan over the meadow until they were gazing into the deep, dark recesses of the trees. Trifan shivered as a chill breeze brushed his face.

"When one lives so near to the forest, you cannot help but hear of her legends," murmured Tumlinfay. "If I were to tell you all of her tales, we would be standing here until covered in snow!"

Trifan thought he saw a pained expression cross the magician's face, as though a sudden memory had been rekindled.

"The tale I am about to tell happened not far from here, though it was many years ago, in the year 745, during the reign of Queen Ellawene. It concerns a young knight called Girlion Fairhead, from the Royal House of Flax. It tells of his quest for a love that would torment him until his death."

Trifan looked up at the magician curiously and then at the dark trees.

"It was one fine September day," continued Tumlinfay, "When Girlion set off from his village in the south of Fluxen, to journey to a jousting tournament on the other side Whitewebbs. His long route took him through the resplendent autumn shades of red, brown and gold following an old woodland track, used only by foresters and mushroom-traders, those that were not terrified of venturing into Whitewebbs." Tumlinfay paused as the sound of a woodpecker took to the air. The magician then continued. "His journey would take him many days travelling and so as a precaution he loaded a week's supply of food and sacks of water upon the back of his father's donkey. During the first day, he saw no one, hearing only the hoot of a tawny owl from above.

"The second day was the same but as afternoon turned to dusk and the light began to grow steadily worse, the track suddenly narrowed until the trees on either side grew up with their branches forming into an archway. Soon, he found his way was blocked, with clinging tentacles of bramble forming into an impenetrable barrier. Dismounting from his horse, he drew his sword and began to hack a path through the thorns. He cut and slashed until both arms ached and then to his relief he came upon a clearing.

"In the middle of that open space was a pool of water and by its side a statue of a young maiden carved in stone. "How strange," he thought.

"That night Girlion made camp beneath the mysterious statue and ate a frugal supper. The following morning dawned chill and he flinched as he glanced up and found the maiden had disappeared. In a panic, he also realised his horse, donkey and supplies had been stolen. Then, as he frantically searched the edge of the thicket, he heard his name being softly called in the haunting voice of a young lady and as the autumn leaves began to fall at his feet, he saw the lady who had called out his name. Girlion stood in shock as the maiden swept toward him, her long gown of autumn shades trailing in the leaves. Her hair was golden- red and her eyes a sparkling green and in her smile, there was a radiance that bewitched him like a dream. They kissed and Girlion was lost in love, enchanted by the wonder before his eyes. She said not a word but put a finger to his lips and beckoned him to follow. Deeper and deeper into the woods they wandered, holding hands like children lost and through the trees, a warm wind blew, like the last of summer's breath. Then they lay together entwined, like two creatures of the forest. Girlion spoke to her on whispered breath and asked the woman her name.

"I am a sommerling of the woods," her answer came so sweet. "Faylenseth is my name and one who loves you, dear. As seasons change, so will I and for one whole year I shall stay by your side but when autumn returns the following year, so I shall be gone from your life."

"He did not heed her words as he lay trapped within her spell and so side by side they wandered far, learning the secrets of the trees. The animals and birds became their friends, as deep in love they came to be. Soon autumn passed to winter's fold and wrapped in furs they pressed each other close. Snows came and then melted under a lingering sun and then came spring's sweet scent upon green-tipped buds and flowers of blue. To meadows new they wandered, far from Whitewebbs' arms and on pastures new lay down in sweet-smelling grass. Summer's time came hither at last. Watching butterflies dancing high, Faylenseth made Girlion a crown of flowers and laughter touched their hearts.

"Then the long summer nights came to pass and the greensward turned to golden-brown. So, under falling leaves, they travelled far, down to a rolling river, under a night of sparkling stars.

"By the bank, they came to rest and in Faylenseth's eyes a tear of doom did run, not mortal sorrow but of a sommerling broken heart; a love doomed to wander forever alone. So side by side they fell asleep under a blanket of autumn leaves. "Farewell, my mortal love," she sighed, as she stroked his fine beard. "The year has gone and so have I."

"When morning broke, Girlion awoke, rubbed his eyes and looked around. Faylenseth was nowhere to be seen. His love had finally left him. 'Faylenseth! Faylenseth!' he forever cried out her name but no answer came, only the rustle of leaves in the wind. Under trees of old, he wandered far looking for his beloved, to places where they had often been but now no longer tarried."

Tumlinfay took a deep breath and cast a pained look at Whitewebbs. "He never did find his fair Faylenseth, his sommerling-bride. His heart had been pierced a thousand times."

Trifan stood entranced. "It is so sad, whatever became of him?"

"For all we know he wandered forever," answered Tumlinfay, "Through Whitewebbs' ancient trees, a prisoner of his dreams."

"For where shall I search for you in autumn's glow?
Where our dreams lie sheltering in winter's cold.
Our hearts shall warm to spring's sweet beginning,
As we lie on summer meadows bathed in gold."

"That, alas, is the tale of Girlion and Faylenseth."

"Would you mind if I explored Whitewebbs this afternoon?" asked Trifan. A sense of adventure had suddenly gripped him.

"As long as you are back before supper," replied Tumlinfay somewhat concerned. "Stick to the path, my path and take Rosewene."

Tumlinfay and the boy turned away from the forest's edge and walked back to Golenwood.

From a sturdy branch, behind a curtain of willow leaves, a keen pair of eyes watched them leave the meadow. The eyes were curious and were drawn to the tall youth with the straw-coloured hair. She sighed.

The old mortal's house was well known in the outer gardens, once a place where, as night fell, great mischief and merry-making would take place. It was said that the mortal brought good luck, for once he had been seduced by a nymph, many years before and survived. It was then that he had built the straw-house by the forest's edge, near to the gate of Noominglade, hoping, just hoping, he would see his beloved again, such a famous sommerling legend.

She sighed again, such a sad, yet beautiful tale.

The slender figure sneezed and placed a hand to her mouth. "You're too dusty for me old willow tree!"

She dropped from the branch and crept over to the thick hedge. She could still smell their lingering presence. Only one for sure was mortal. Her gaze wandered over the field of white daisies to the long low house, with its crooked, smoking turret.

Who was the newcomer, the tall youth? Maybe tonight she would find her answers. She would creep through the gardens once more and take a peep through the glass.

11

A Sommerling Gift

THAT afternoon as Tumlinfay and Sirifix were in the main parlour sleeping off a heavy dinner, Trifan made his move. Following the magician's instructions, he walked the narrow path that ran alongside a chattering brook.

Soon, he was standing at a small wooden gate that opened out into the vastness of the forest. All was still but for a soft breeze that stroked his face. For a moment he hesitated, unsure, then opened the creaking gate and entered a secret, green world.

It was a tangled forest of oak trees, some young, most old and incredibly gnarled; their hoary trunks were cloaked in thick clumps of moss and straggling ivy. He remembered Tumlinfay's words. "Be warned! not all trees are friendly, some will try and harm you! Whitewebbs is full of rotten trees of malcontent."

Trifan unsheathed Rosewene and gazed upon her form, the sword, at first dull, suddenly sparkled from the hilt to the tip of the blade. Would she reappear to him? But no, the blade returned to its dull form. Trifan sighed heavily and re-sheathed her.

The path through the trees wound on, no plant or flower encroached upon its narrow space. After a while he became aware of the sound of falling water, not the brook he had wandered from but a new sensation, stronger and more powerful.

"Surely, if I walk a few yards from the path, it will be safe," he thought.

He left the path, climbed a small bank and clambered over the writhing roots of an oak tree. A shaft of the sun suddenly blinded his eyes, causing him to trip and stumble down through a bed of ferns until he came to rest at the edge of a small clearing.

He breathed in the heady scents and marvelled at this new sight. "What an enchanting place."

At the far end of the clearing there ran another stream, this one swifter, almost musical to the ears and as he listened he could hear the faint cry of a waterfall. "Think I will stretch out for a while," he said with a yawn. The scent in the air was so intoxicating he had a sudden urge to fall asleep. Trifan's dream was wild and haunted. Where once there had been sunlight, now the shadows began to creep. Suddenly, two dark hands came up from the ground and pinned him against the earth. The hands then slowly elongated into arms and then grotesquely into a gnarled, twisted body. A hideous head then clicked into position and smiled his way, while the clicking of sharp, pointed teeth moved ever nearer to his face.

Trifan reached for Rosewene but a hand wrenched it from his grasp. He cried aloud waiting for his doom, then a clear, high voice pierced the air and the ghoul slithered back into the ground. Trifan lay there bathed in sweat and shaking in terror.

"Awake! For you have slept here long enough, stranger!" commanded the voice.

Trifan rubbed his eyes and looked up, straining his eyes in the deepening gloom. He gasped, as he noticed a small hunched figure resting on a log only a few feet away.

The figure extended a small pair of clear wings and floated down from the log to stand before the startled boy. It was dressed as if it belonged to the forest itself, in shades of green and brown.

Trifan flinched and used his elbows to move backwards in a blind panic.

The tiny creature was barely knee-high, male in appearance and obviously a sommerling. He had a very sharp face and looked decidedly ragged, not from the picture books of Trifan's childhood.

"Who are you?" hissed the creature as he sensed the boy's unease. "Did you know that you fell asleep within an enchanted glade?"

"No, sorry if I offended you," stuttered the boy, still reeling in shock.

The creature's voice softened upon hearing the apology, he almost felt sorry for the mortal.

"Not all parts of the forest are safe, especially here at Nim, a dark place to rest." He poked his sharp face nearer to the boy.

"Did your foolish sleep by the stream please and refresh you, or did it torment and trick you?"

Trifan was lost for words, he had never seen a sommerling before, let alone talk to one. He felt clumsy and oafish.

"Well?" pressed the sommerling.

"When I fell asleep I had a nightmare," confessed Trifan. "If you hadn't stirred me I..."

"You would have succumbed to the magic of Nim, never to awake. The heavy scent in the air and the music of the water enticed you." The creature then smiled a little. "I saw you enter the woods. No doubt you have come from the old mortal's house?"

Trifan laughed at the description of Tumlinfay as he looked down in wonder at the creature before him, a slight figure with darting green eyes and a thatch of long, dirty fair hair; while over his shoulder hung a leather pouch.

"I hope you've learnt your lesson," he sighed, his clear voice tinged with disappointment. He then thrust his hand upward, with long fingers extended. "My name is Wilfin. Wilfin Twoflute but just call me Wilfin."

"I am Trifan. Trifan Foxley," replied the boy, as he touched the sommerling's hand.

Wilfin's face creased into a smile. "Unusual name, still I don't meet many mortals."

"Are you a sommerling of these woods?" asked Trifan, still shaking, as if he had been thrown into a cold river.

Wilfin laughed aloud. "Maybe I am, maybe I'm not." The creature pulled back his curling, fair hair to reveal large pointed ears. "I think that is obvious now." He then tapped his leather pouch. "I haven't come this far west to discuss my ears but to collect water from Eldris."

The sommerling then paused and began to look Trifan up and down; whereupon his long nimble fingers began to inspect the boy's clothing before dropping to stroke the scabbard that held Rosewene. Suddenly, the sommerling pulled his hand back.

"You have a fine sword for one so young," he murmured softly.

Trifan unsheathed Rosewene and held her up before the startled eyes of the small creature.

Wilfin reached up again with eager fingers but then withdrew them and looked away as though in a distant thought. Trifan noticed a tear in his eye. "How strange," whispered Wilfin, "How very strange." He turned and fixed the boy with glistening eyes. "I too hear news outside these borders. But if you have come from the old man's house and possess a fine sword then maybe this dread we face concerns you?"

"I feel I have sleepwalked into a nightmare," replied

Trifan sadly. "It is such a heavy weight to carry. I am only a gardener."

"Then it appears we can both do with a drink from Eldris!" exclaimed Wilfin. "Come, we shall follow the stream deeper into the forest, yes, deeper we go."

Trifan followed without fear. Soon they began to climb a narrow path where the trees and abundant ferns clung to the bank, rooted near to the enchanted waters. Then, as the path levelled, Wilfin brushed aside an overhanging willow branch and they both came across a wondrous sight and as if by magic the noise of the tumbling water suddenly came to the fore. Rising before them to at least thirty feet was a moss-covered shelf of rock, itself as green as the surrounding forest. The water, though clear and sparkling, dropped in a single curtain of white, spraying the ferns and overhanging branches. The water seemed to sing as it cascaded upon shards of rock, or poured gurgling into the many channels and deep pools. "The Falls of Eldris!" cried Wilfin excitedly, as he leapt upon a rock in the middle of the chattering stream. The green cliff loomed large above the sommerling. "What an enchanting song she sings, much safer than old Nim, there only the dark spirits of dryads linger."

Wilfin spread his wings, embraced the spray and leapt from the rock to the flower-strewn bank. He scratched his long, dirty hair and then plunged it into the water. "Best bath you can have," he chuckled.

Before Trifan could blink, Wilfin was before him looking

up at him curiously. "Something strange is happening, for sure. Perhaps, the Prince of the Sommerlings will rise once more."

Trifan crouched down before the creature. "What do you mean?"

The sommerling placed a finger to his lips. "Throughout the spring these gardens, this Galadris, our garden, is more silent, the birds do not sing." Trifan listened. The only sound was the beautiful, yet lonely song of falling water.

"Rumours of a dark dread have surfaced once more. Soon, not just the hidden lands but mortal Elbion will be doomed." Wilfin's voice lowered and he looked suddenly to the twisted trunks of the forest, sensing that maybe the evil already lurked within. "It is said that goblins are walking abroad, uglier than the ugliest mortal and feasting on small animals and birds. During the day, they crawl into the hollows of rocks or tree roots. They are waiting to be gathered once again, waiting for the call of Grib." Trifan gasped in terror and a shadow covered his heart.

The sound of tumbling water came to the fore again. A spell had broken.

"Let us drink from the pool!" exclaimed Wilfin in a sudden cheery voice. He opened his pouch and scooped up the clear water. "Open your hands Trifan and taste the magic of Eldris."

The water tasted sweet and his mood lightened. Before he knew what he was doing, he found he had stretched out upon the flower-strewn bank, with Wilfin kneeling by his side. Soon, Trifan was telling the wandering sommerling of his days in Oakendale to Tumlinfay's arrival and their sudden flight to Golenwood.

Wilfin, who was chewing upon a blade of grass, looked at the boy with a changing face of expressions, as each episode was told. In the end, he sat up and moved nearer to the boy.

"Our paths have crossed and I am pleased. I have so many questions to fire your way, to ask them all would last a day." The sommerling fidgeted uneasily. "Your tale is far darker than I could imagine and your words have chilled me to the bone." Wilfin ran a thin hand along the tip of Rosewene. "So she is the sommerling elf I could sense all along. Her magic does indeed run deep." He sighed and withdrew his trembling hand. "These gardens are no place to feast, or dance now, their magic is on the wane. The shadow has arrived, even here at Eldris." The sound of water faded into the background as though it belonged to another world. Then Wilfin spoke quietly. "It is not for mortal ears to know such things, for mortal tongue a danger brings, yet you have trusted me in such a way, a name I'll give to pass the day." Trifan breathed deeply and sat entranced. "King Barcorn waits behind the gate, it's time to leave, it's getting late." Wilfin knew that he would be punished if he revealed any more. He knew the spies of Grib would be waiting. "Barcorn is our king, ruler of all the Sommerlands. That, my mortal, is where we go when our wanderings are done and we want to go home."

"The Sommerlands," gasped Trifan. "Where is it, where does it lie?"

"There are many doors that lead us home," answered Wilfin softly. "You are near one now. But we are all being called home, for soon the doors to our land will be shut forever!"

Wilfin glanced to the trees. "That is our only way to keep danger at bay." The sound of Eldris suddenly returned as if having returned from banishment.

"Let me give you a parting gift," said Wilfin. He reached into his ragged cloak, retrieved an object and placed it carefully in the boy's outstretched palm. Trifan looked down and saw a tiny wooden pipe.

"It is a flute, an ancient flute," added Wilfin. "If you are in danger, just press the flute to your lips and a tune shall follow."

Trifan put it to his lips.

"No, no!" Wilfin tugged his sleeve, "Only when you are in danger. It is old, it is dusty. Please, tuck it away for now."

Trifan noticed it was dusk, yet the only sound was the music of the falls. There was no birdsong.

"Reminds me," said Wilfin, "Better fill the sack or I will be in trouble." The sommerling filled the leather pouch with water and slung it over his shoulder.

"Well, Trifan Foxley, it is time to say goodbye." He

wiped a tear from his eye. "Good luck with your strange task. Hopefully, on a clear night when Morgalene is slain, Rosewene shall be re-united with Eldsmoreth and you with your beloved rose gardens." He gazed up at the boy fondly. "Now it is time to go home."

Before Trifan could blink, Wilfin, with his bag of water, had swiftly turned and darted into the ferns behind them, leaving no trace of movement and no sound.

Trifan was left alone marvelling up at the falls of Eldris. Though unknown to him another pair of eyes were watching him from the dense trees on the other side of the stream.

It was another wandering sommerling, one who had watched him by the meadow. How he had intrigued her, how she wanted to be near him, look into his eyes.

As Trifan walked back through the trees and eventually back along the path to Golenwood, she began to follow, creeping barefoot through the lengthening shadows. The trees recognised her scent and moved aside their ancient branches and writhing roots. "Ah, Ninfa," they sighed, "Sweet Ninfa."

After his encounter with Wilfin, Trifan set about scouring Tumlinfay's vast collection of books, for information regarding the fabled Sommerlands; but there was no mention, no records, neither was there mention of a king called Barcorn.

The temptation to tell the magician he had spoken to a

sommerling was strong but an inner voice told him to remain silent.

12

The Secret Door

THAT night a deep and peaceful sleep comforted Trifan. His dream still lingered in the secret realm of the sommerlings as the morning's soft light crept through the cracks in the window-shutters and bathed his face. Trifan opened an eye and saw that he was resting upon a bed of goose feathers, not lying under a blanket of autumn leaves.

For a moment, he thought of running away from the magician and returning to Oakendale.

"Not thinking of leaving for your gardens, I hope?"

Trifan turned to his side and saw Tumlinfay smiling at him from the leather chair. "One day you will return I promise but you have another path to follow, Trifan, you cannot give up yet!"

"I know I cannot return," whispered the boy. "But it feels I am losing my past for a future I don't yet understand."

"That is how I felt when I inherited my legacy," confessed Tumlinfay. "I am sure Rosewene will win your heart in time, as Eldsmoreth did with me. Soon we shall be planning our task that is set for Mistletoe Eve, three days from now. The time for play is coming to an end."

Trifan yawned and sat up in bed.

Tumlinfay strode over the creaking boards and opened the shutters, letting the morning sun stream in. Outside, the birds were singing and the bees settling upon the lavender heads. Perhaps Golenwood was the last safe enclave for wildlife.

In his heart, Trifan felt sadness, doubt and a little fear.

"On Mistletoe Eve, my companions will arrive," said Tumlinfay, settling back into the chair. "They will help us decide which path to follow."

"Are they magicians, like you?" asked Trifan.

"Yes, we are the remnants from the ancient order of Garfax," replied Tumlinfay. "The last magicians of Elbion. Now we are regarded as fayreground conjurors and quacks; but our power still remains, much to the annoyance of the Church." A smile crossed his lips.

"After my departure in May, I sent letters to the remaining five in our order. First, I informed Proudsickle, our esteemed head, informing him of my discovery of Rosewene and Eldsmoreth and the sacred gardens of Liminulin. I told him of the quest to be undertaken, to seek out and slay Morgalene."

Trifan breathed deeply and felt incredibly powerless.

"I summoned a 'Gathering', the first of its kind in fifty years," continued the magician. "As head of our order,

Proudsickle sent messengers to old acquaintances, most not seen for many a year, but dear friends, all the same; namely, Rumbleweed, Bedevere, Mordegan and Windlesax," Tumlinfay's voice trailed away. He knew Mordegan lived far away in the Hills of Belf, while Windlesax lived in the wilds of Ildonia. Bedevere would definitely attend, also Rumbleweed, who needed a new purpose after his seduction by a sommerling.

Mordegan, though secretive, would attend but Windlesax was getting on in years and much too old for a task such as this.

Trifan climbed from his bed, he was sure Rosewene had warmed against his thigh.

Tumlinfay suddenly laughed aloud, as he observed the gangly youth, standing in his crumpled nightwear, with the sword strapped to his bare leg. "You, my lad, will do yourself an injury!" The boy's face reddened.

"Anyhow, you are on your own today," smiled the magician, "So no wandering, no snooping and no mischief making!"

"But where are you going?" asked Trifan in surprise. The thought of being alone bothered him.

"I will be securing the outer fields and meadows around Golenwood, while Sirifix has already left for supplies from the market in Hautinwyx." The magician bowed to the boy and turned to leave the room. "You will find tea on the stove and plenty of books to read, good day to you!"

With that, the heavy oak door ground shut.

Trifan knew that until this 'Gathering', the magician was keeping many secrets from him. He had no choice but to trust him. Though the house was warm and inviting, not too dark, or too light, Trifan sensed that it too held many secrets; secrets that it was not about to share. As he made his inquisitive way from room to room, he began to find that cupboards wouldn't open for him, even if the key were turned, or that doors would mysteriously creak shut behind him as if a sudden breeze had stroked the heavy bracketed wood.

If the cottage was supposedly his friendly haven, it had a strange way of showing it. If maybe, he was a little more superstitious, he would have guessed the ancient dwelling was haunted. But he knew deep down that ghosts weren't the cause of unease and mischief, it was the house itself. It was watching his every move!

Before he knew it, he heard a faint voice ushering him downstairs and soon he was left standing in the hall, outside the library door. The latch to the room clicked upward but try as he might the door wouldn't shift. Before him the front door to the porch and gardens beyond had opened, politely grinning at him, almost instructing him to step outside.

Taking one last look at the long hallway, he was sure the suit of armour had moved and then, as he lingered on the threshold, the grandfather clock chimed loudly and the heavy oak door, which had been swaying impatiently upon its creaking hinges, suddenly closed from the inside, pushing him off balance and out into the porch, before slamming shut behind him. Trifan lay on the ground in stunned silence. Golenwood had come alive and then thrown him out, like an unwanted lodger!

He thumped upon the front door and pushed with all his might but the door held firm. From inside, he could hear many triumphant chimes from the clock and the faint ethereal sound of muted laughter.

Trifan backed away from the porch and looked up at the cottage in disbelief. The sturdy old house appeared to be smiling back at him, with its sparkling clear windows, gaping mouth of a porch and thick mop of golden thatch. "Too nice a day to be indoors anyhow!" he called out while rubbing his knee.

No reply came, just a strong breeze which rustled the tall flower-heads and clusters of reeds that crowded the brook. He closed his eyes, breathed in the heady air and with a whistle upon his lips, turned and so followed the pathway that led to the gated opening of Whitewebbs. As he approached, the open arms of oak trees swooped down as if to greet him, beckoning him to enter the glade.

It was almost as if Golenwood and its gardens were an extension of the forest itself.

With the sun on his back, he opened the small, creaking gate and entered the cool gloom of the tangled trees. Though the way was familiar, he could sense that it had altered, something was amiss; where trees had grown the previous day, there appeared a gap, strewn now only with ferns and holly bushes. Like the mysterious cottage, he knew that this vast collection of trees had a life of its own. He had also studied the magician's many detailed maps and marvelled how he could leave Golenwood and walk all the way to the East Downs and never once leave the shadows of the trees.

Not far into the forest, the once broad path gradually narrowed and then, to his alarm, stopped at a dead end. Thick ferns formed a high scented barrier, fanning out from one gnarled oak tree to another. He knew his brief adventure had come to an abrupt end. It was not a forest about to share its many secrets. He knew he would never find the beautiful Eldris again. Suddenly, he heard the strangest of sounds, what appeared to be the turning of a key in a lock and then the slow grind of a heavy door. The sound came to his right, from where a lop-sided oak grinned at him, with a huge beard of thick, curling ivy.

Trifan instinctively crouched down within the sweet-smelling ferns, looking on in shock as the ivy moved outward from the trunk! It revealed not only the clinging tendrils of cobwebs but the tall magician himself, dressed entirely in dark green, from the tip of his pointed broad-rimmed hat to the thick cloak that swept around his ankles.

The door of ivy appeared to grind shut. The magician looked swiftly to his left and right and vanished into the sea of surrounding ferns.

Trifan's breathing quickened and his mind began to race. Had Tumlinfay found a door to the Sommerlands?

Wilfin had after all disclosed the secret of his sommerling-bride. But why had he kept it secret from him, if, as he had said, the doors would be closing forever. Why wouldn't Tumlinfay lead them all to safety?

For a brief moment, he wondered if he had trusted his life to a madman, for whatever Tumlinfay was up to, he certainly wasn't securing the outer fields and meadows.

Could he trust the old magician again?

Trifan rose and glanced over to where the magician had disappeared. He noticed that the ferns remained flattened. A warm breeze then stroked his face and swiftly drew his attention to the lop-sided tree and its secret door; inviting him to draw near. Was this the sommerling-door Wilfin had spoken about?

Reaching through the ivy stems he could feel the roughness, not of wood but of stone. It was a stone door, set within the broad trunk of an oak tree. Trifan tried to wedge his fingers into the large, oval groove but the stone held firm. Carefully, he lifted the leaves and found a deep diamond-shaped hole, where a thick key would have slotted. He let the curtain of ivy fall. "Well I never," he whispered. He smiled to himself. He knew that Tumlinfay possessed two keys, one for Golenwood and one for this mysterious door. He also knew he kept them hanging on a hook from a beam in the kitchen. The urge to see into the unknown surged through his veins.

Just then, he heard the clear sound of a bell, followed by the faint voice of Sirifix calling him home for tea.

13

The Magpie
and the Letter

IT was early on Thursday evening, just two days before Mistletoe Eve, when Trifan and the magicians were resting in the main parlour, having just finished a fine supper.

Sirifix and the boy were playing cards, while Tumlinfay sat by the fire sucking upon a long clay pipe.

He was still waiting to hear from his friends. "I'm surprised we haven't heard from Bedevere," he said anxiously.

Sirifix looked up baffled. "I agree, he was a most curious fellow after all. You remember how the legend of Grizilder gripped Garfax, until the great fire of 1035 destroyed all of the manuscripts. This quest would have tempted him."

Tumlinfay drew upon his pipe but remained silent. He had been too wrapped up in his own world to care about his former friends or the Order. Only his loyal friend Sirifix had kept him sane.

Despite the time of year, the once sweltering summer had given way to an unexplained chill, so much so that the magician had stoked the inglenook and tossed last year's logs upon the fire. His mood appeared grim. Trifan watched as the flames danced and licked within the large hearth. It was then that he noticed an unusual object set upon the cross-beam of the fire. It appeared to be an image of a man's melancholy face staring out from a thick cluster of leaves.

"What is the face above the fire, Tumlinfay?"

The magician rose from the chair and gazed with fondness at his old friend. "That, my boy, is a mask of summer. He goes by the name of Nuner, a spirit of summer. He has been with me for many years."

Tumlinfay smiled to himself. It was, he thought, too early to reveal the truth. Trifan had never seen anything so beautiful, yet so terrifying at the same time. "What does it mean?" asked the boy in wonder. "It looks like a death-mask." He was sure he had seen something similar before, set within the old Abbey stonework.

"It is an ancient symbol," said Sirifix, who proceeded to drain a glass of wine in one and then belch loudly. "It represents the awesome power of nature."

Tumlinfay frowned at his friend's coarseness. Still, the magician could not reveal the truth. He hoped his friends would forgive him one day.

Trifan was sure the face had moved a little, like fluid

set within a mould; or maybe it was a reflection from the fire. "Can I touch it?" asked the boy.

"Definitely not, young man," replied the magician swiftly. "There is a power within the mask that even I have yet to understand."

Trifan sat beguiled by the mask, which he was sure now smiled at him. "Nuner," he sighed.

Suddenly, there came a faint tapping at the front door. Sirifix rose from an armchair with his bottle and ambled slowly to the hallway. "Unexpected guests at this late hour."

As Sirifix opened the door, he was instantly met with the sudden chill of an early winter and then the strange sight of an enormous magpie, skipping over the threshold and then hobbling ungainly into the hall.

"A hop-leg!" exclaimed Sirifix, as he took a swig from the bottle and then looked on in amazement as the creature cocked its head at its warmer surroundings and the three startled occupants.

The bird smiled; it had done its job to perfection. In his beak, he gripped a waxed, rolled parchment that had been written only two days previously, in a tower far away, in a manor-house called Grendeline.

Tumlinfay knew the author but was surprised at his choice of messenger; for magpies had an evil reputation as a bird of ill-omen. "Proudsickle's reply on time," said the magician.

The magpie locked a cold yellow eye upon the old man

who sat by the fire and remembered the message from his master. It skipped nonchalantly past Sirifix and for a fleeting moment, looked up at the boy before cocking its giant head and shuffling off towards the pointed slippers of Tumlinfay; whereupon it tossed the parchment at the magician's feet. It then cawed loudly in its harsh language, before resting a little and opening its broad wings to the warmth of the fire.

"Whatever happened to the doves," muttered Sirifix, feeling vexed at being ignored. "At least they would always wait politely in the hall, unlike this hop-leg."

Trifan laughed aloud as the large magpie hopped around and cast the plump magician an evil glare.

Tumlinfay unrolled the parchment and recognised Proudsickle's fine, feathery handwriting. He also noticed the strange prose, rambling and excitable.

Tumlinfay cleared his throat and read the script out aloud.

Tumlinfay   *Proudsickle*
Golenwood   *Grendeline Manor*
Fluxen   *Year 1071*

Subject: My long-awaited arrival at Golenwood

To my dear brother Tum (or to bestow upon you your rightful name, Tumlinfay, Tum-of-the-magic).

Please accept my new messenger, Tarak. He is highly

intelligent and can understand our tongue. He can be temperamental but is far surer, far swifter than those accursed doves; which were easy prey for the hawks of 'Whitewebbs'!

To think brother, you have not only unearthed Eldsmoreth (from a ditch near Garfax), all those years ago but have also harnessed his power to awaken the sleeping Rosewene, a name also dear to my heart.

It has been a long time since our last correspondence and you appear to have been a lot busier than me. Ha ha, always ahead of the game, eh? A man of many secrets. As you know, I have been busy at my stables at Grendeline but I still harbour a deep, deep interest in the Sommerlands. It has been a long time since we studied elven-lore at school but now I consider myself a star pupil!

I too have seen behind the veil; opened a door into that blessed realm. I have at last conversed with sommerlings and seen sights that would truly beguile and shock you. I think I have a name at last for that magical realm. I could write deep into the night upon our, your discovery. My, my, I still cannot believe how close we are to this wondrous, incredible mystery. It all makes sense now, the pieces are joining together; how Eldsmoreth fled north with Rosewene on his saddle, how he caressed her for the last time, then buried her deep within the soils of Liminulin (Oakendale, dear boy) and then fled northwards again from Morgalene, vowing one day to return.

To think then his doom took place near Garfax, in a

deep, lonely ditch. How I must have passed that place many times on my travels.

I wholeheartedly agree to a 'Gathering' on Mistletoe Eve. As yet, I cannot locate our brothers, Bedevere, Mordegan, Rumbleweed, or Windlesax but I have dispatched messengers to them, as requested.

(I think though, alas, that poor Rumbleweed has finally been driven to madness over the nymph, Forswain.) I shall arrive as planned; with some new companions, recent friends and then we can plan our next move.

We must act swiftly, for Morgalene is now walking abroad. She is coming for us, my friend and she is coming for the boy!

PS Do not attempt to leave, Tum-of-the-magic, stay put until we arrive.

High regards, Proudsickle

Tumlinfay did not read out the last paragraph.

Tumlinfay and Sirifix stared at one another, as the fire crackled loudly. "This is dire news, most alarming," pondered Sirifix. "Perhaps Rumbleweed has finally fallen into madness. Bedevere also is not the magician he used to be. When I last saw him two years ago, he was in poor shape, scrawny and drunk! Neither has been seen in five years, no letters, nothing."

Tumlinfay nodded while sucking upon his clay pipe.

"Mordegan is reclusive now," continued Sirifix. "He

never writes, just lives alone in his manor, deep in the Belf Hills. You'll never draw that old badger out of his deep sett."

"True, true," said Tumlinfay. "What about Windlesax? He was very learned in sommerling-lore, he would adore this tale."

"He is getting too old, Tum, as we all are," replied Sirifix. "He's twice my age. He would struggle through the valleys of Ildonia to get here." Sirifix thought for a moment. "I have an ill-feeling of this, that letter was tinged with, well, madness. It's as if Proudsickle is possessed. Can you believe that he even sent out messengers, as you requested."

"I can't see why he wouldn't," replied Tumlinfay. "You shouldn't let old grievances cloud the issue. We shall wait for Proudsickle. We can trust his skill and judgement."

"And his new 'companions'," mocked Sirifix, "I wouldn't be surprised if he arrived with Morgalene herself for tea!"

Tumlinfay frowned at his friend.

The fire crackled loudly again in the background. It was then that they noticed the ugly magpie had vanished, though a strange odour remained.

14

The Green Bottle

THE lone rider cantered along the empty country lane. It was early evening and the fruitfulness of summer had a distinct chill in the air. He had travelled this road many times in the past, no doubt in merrier times, from his house in the east.

The road was long and followed the northern tip of Whitewebbs' ancient boughs; sometimes meandering into its murky green depths. It passed through small hamlets, numerous taverns and hunting lodges; but it was a road that was getting less well-travelled as the year progressed. He smiled at that thought, for he knew the reason why.

He patted the small casket that hung from the side of the saddle, always aware of the power within. Luckily, his mount Askalon, was less nervous than before; just a few words in his ear and a choice batch of oats did the trick.

This time, he planned to finish the job, how he had squandered the power of the white bottles, such a gift for grander times. He was angry, angry and tired, as the wretched road pressed on and the twinkling lights of farmsteads gradually faded away.

Then he saw a familiar turning to the left, a high steep bank drenched with primroses and a narrow rutted lane that wound its way to Golenwood. At last, he was there. He nudged Askalon and led him down the steeply banked lane. The sweet-scented primrose and pungent cow-parsley brought back happier memories but alas, it would all have to go!

It wasn't long until he had passed over the dainty white bridge and came to stop outside Tumlinfay's retreat.

At the entrance, there was a high, wooden gate, with a tiled roof, set between a thick impenetrable hedge of holly. The path beyond, which was lined with large white stones, meandered through a bountiful orchard of pears.

Proudsickle sniffed the rich, hazy air. Still, the perfume of mid-summer lingered, yet it was chill.

"The snows await your command," croaked the hideous voice of Morgalene inside his head. He placed a flat hand to his aching forehead. "Once the grey bottles are broken," she hissed, "Our new realm shall begin to take shape." A harsh cackle made him cry out and Askalon rear up.

Morgalene's voice faded into the emptiness of the night. Proudsickle shivered, pulled his cloak tighter and dropped from the saddle. The sky above, though grey, was tinged with a strange pink hue. He had no time to lose, it was now, or never. He unstrapped the leather catches at the side of the saddle, pulled the box free and with a curiosity surging through his body, swiftly opened the lid.

Inside, were the last of Morgalene's gifts, these were two medium-sized grey bottles and one large green bottle. He removed his riding gloves and with the green bottle in his right hand, tilted it to and fro noticing that inside slopped and lapped a ghastly fluid of some sort.

Morgalene stayed silent, his headache had left him.

"Charming abode, my friend, most charming." Proudsickle tethered Askalon and with the box in both hands, passed through the gate and on into the orchards, calmly walking past the ancient pear trees and up into the high gardens of ferns and leafy rock-pools.

Golenwood was an ancient place, one that he wished to possess. For it had magical qualities that some say linked it to the sommerling world itself, a portal to their hidden realm.

Proudsickle smiled and breathed deeply, for Tum would never tell him its secrets.

Suddenly, there was a harsh croak from an over-hanging tree branch. The sorcerer looked up and then held out his palm. Tarak dropped down and rested upon his sleeve. "Well?" asked Proudsickle, as he studied the magpie closely.

The ugly bird cackled and rasped a reply.

"I see, just the three of them; the wizard, the boy and a rather rude fat man," laughed Proudsickle, "All soon to be deceased."

"Grah! Grah!" laughed Tarak.

"Yes, my friend, dead, dead!"

Inside the cottage, Sirifix peered from the curtains and looked out into the deepening gloom. "I heard a noise coming from the orchards, I'm sure." Tumlinfay looked up from his book. "Maybe our friend has arrived early, Proudsickle always liked to surprise."

Trifan tiptoed to the kitchen. For some inexplicable reason, he reached up to the beam above the stove, the one with the dried herbs and after fingering around, took down a pair of keys. Putting a set in his tunic pocket, he returned the other to the hook.

"Ah, I wondered where you were."

Trifan turned and saw the tall frame of Tumlinfay standing in the doorway. "Come, my boy, it's better we stay together."

Proudsickle lowered Tarak to the grass and then proceeded to open the box. He took out the two grey bottles.

Tarak watched closely, his beady, yellow eye noticing that each bottle contained a swirling mist of some sort. Proudsickle examined one of them, first sniffing it then holding it to his ear.

From the inside of the glass he could hear the faintest of sounds, like a ripple of thunder, or the patter of heavy rain, he wasn't quite sure. Tarak croaked with excitement.

"Once the bottles are broken, their doom is set." These were Morgalene's words. "Winter's fury shall descend and summer shall be entombed." Proudsickle lifted a bottle in both hands and for a moment held them high above his head; before him stood the pretty thatched house of Tumlinfay, its soft lights twinkling and before the house, the rich fragrant gardens, all in the full bloom of summer.

There was still time to turn, to replace the bottles. Ah! How his arms ached. His head spun, as the magic of Golenwood went to work on him. "No, no, no!" he cried, "My magic is stronger!"

Proudsickle's voice changed, its menace and venom forced Tarak to the nearest branch.

"I am the winter wizard, all power to me!"

Proudsickle smashed the glass bottles upon a broad slab of slate, sending out plumes of thick, billowing smoke, that swelled and expanded upward and outward but before he could shield his eyes, the clouds of smoke gathered together to form into one swirling, spiral pole, that roared skyward, disappearing into the early evening sky.

Proudsickle staggered back, shocked at the power he had unleashed. He gazed open-mouthed to the skies above. There remained the pinky hue tinge of a summer's sky. He had failed again! How was that possible, were they to break in a special way?

Suddenly, he shivered violently, as then the sky darkened rapidly, pink fading to slate-grey. There came an almighty roar and then absolute silence.

Proudsickle sniffed the air and smiled. First, the intricate scents of summer began to vanish, then the sounds, the small unnoticed sounds, of crickets, of late bumble-bees and of the blackbird looking for the last tasty morsel. All sounds, the entire myriad of small, yet important signs of summer; simply gone. They had all vanished.

From high above came the first white flakes, beautiful to behold. Proudsickle pulled his cloak tighter and held out his long arms. Snow began to fall upon his palm, on his cloak and boots; it also began to cover the orchard and gardens.

He had learnt of the legend of the winter wizard and knew the power now within his grasp. He picked up the last remaining bottle and turned to look for Tarak. The tiresome hop-leg had vanished, no doubt feasting upon the carcass of a fallen bird or mouse.

As winter took hold over Golenwood, Proudsickle strode up the steps of the rock-garden, clasping the green bottle in his right hand, while his eyes were wide open, slaked with the power unleashed. In only a matter of minutes, the once green countryside was covered under a blanket of snow.

It was then that the summer seemed to draw its last breath. Frantic birds took to the freezing night air, some-times flying for only a brief moment until they dropped dead and fell lifeless to the glistening, white shroud below.

"Oh, how weak is the spirit of summer!" cried Proudsickle.

He strode across the small bridge and stood at last

under the thatched eaves of magical Golenwood. His heart was beating heavily and despite the gnawing cold, sweat lay in beads upon his forehead.

As he paused, he looked once more at the large green bottle, watching with morbid curiosity as the liquid slopped to and fro. He recalled the words of his queen with new gusto.

"My beautiful Dragool. Drink the potion I have bottled for thee, drink!" Proudsickle uncorked the bottle, sniffed its contents and staggered back in revulsion. Then he steadied himself, opened his mouth and drank its foul contents. He threw the empty bottle into the snow-covered gardens, belched loudly and then waited.

What was going to happen to him? What new power? He smiled as he saw the grey bottles unleash their power, as beautiful snow fell all around. He shook his boots and chuckled.

Then the sharp voice of Morgalene entered his head. "You are my dear Dragool, dear Dragool!" she cackled. "Enter the straw house and take the sword and the walking stick. Slay the mortals, slay them all!" Her hideous voice ended in a hiss.

He clutched his head with his long fingers. There was no going back. Proudsickle was no more. He could feel his blood surging through his entire body, never had he felt so alive, so powerful.

It was as if the might of winter's arrival had entered him, swept away his old, mortal self.

He stood before the door to Golenwood, his new height almost touching the ceiling of the porch. With a fist, now tinged with a strange green hue, he pounded the heavy oak door.

"Tumlinfay! Open in the name of Morgalene!"

For a brief moment, there was silence. All Proudsickle could hear was the swirling of blood through his veins; which, he noticed, caused them to expand then settle. As he looked at his large hands, his old self offered a shriek of horror! What had he done? Maybe he was meant to smash the bottle, to release the demon inside, not drink its foul contents! His entire body was turning green!

"But you did drink me," came another voice in his head. "I am, or should I say, we are one. We are now called Dragool. That is what you always wanted."

The figure that was once Proudsickle shrieked in horror then realized he had lost. It was all over; his old self was being consumed. Suddenly, the door creaked ominously open.

Proudsickle looked up and saw two figures standing in the shadowy hall, one tall, very tall: the other short and round. There was no third figure ... the boy. But it was the tall figure that shocked him. For in his right hand was raised the gnarled walking-staff Eldsmoreth, while upon this figure's face, ringed with white hair, was the terrifying mask of Nuner himself.

15

Ninfa

TRIFAN had noticed the snows beginning to fall from the study window. He could feel Rosewene stir at his side, this time the warmth almost began to burn his leg. He flinched and then he saw movement in the gardens beyond, a swift darting figure, too agile to see.

He pulled Sirifix's thick cloak on over his tunic, unlatched the side door and entered the frozen gardens. The cold was a shock, it stung his face and he found it hard to breathe as his lungs pained him.

His boots crunched the snow underfoot, while his right hand gripped the warm hilt of Rosewene. The touch was a welcome relief in this new winter realm. He could hear the frantic voices of Tumlinfay and Sirifix back in the main parlour, one had raised his voice. He stopped and listened, yet he had no intention of going back; something, or someone, lured him on. Suddenly, he saw movement to his left. He stopped and stared at the forest of reedbeds that still lined the river but were now set like silver spears, rising up from a swirling plume of white mist.

Trifan's breathing was heavy and he stumbled clumsily forward. As his eyes narrowed, gazing into the frozen air, he, at last, saw what he wanted to see. She was an elusive creature, peering out from the reeds, a beautiful and beguiling sight, her sharp face framed with a tangled halo of fair hair. He could see her eyes studying him intently.

Then, before he could blink, she had vanished. The reeds swayed, yet there was no breeze and he could hear her swift flight to the forest beyond.

With agility that surprised him, he began his chase running until his legs and lungs ached. "Come back!" he cried, though his voice sounded muffled. "Come back, I won't harm you."

The lone hoot of an owl made him flinch as did the cold touch of tree bark as he stood apprehensively upon the edge of Whitewebbs. Trifan was torn in two, he gazed back to Golenwood, something terrible was happening yet he remained rooted to the spot, he couldn't go back; Tumlinfay was bound to be okay. All lights had been extinguished, the only signs of life were the thin tendrils of smoke, rising upward from the chimney.

As he hesitated, he could hear a hideous roar take to the night air, a ghastly shriek, followed by a sudden loud explosion and a great, billowing purple flame that leapt skyward, before shards of its power splintered and rained down upon the cottage, a place he now loved with all his heart, a place he knew he would never see again.

He held a hand to his mouth and screamed in shock for he could see the purple flames eat away at this most magical abode. He knew the enemy, in whatever form it took, had come.

"Tumlinfay! Sirifix!" he cried.

Then he could hear the magician's voice rising high above the destruction. "To the woods, my boy, to the woods; run!"

Trifan's legs were heavy, he found he couldn't run. Tears welled in his eyes as he saw the destruction of Golenwood. The boy fell to his knees, he was so near the chilling embrace of the forest, yet he squatted in the open. Heavy snow fell all around him and for a brief moment, he closed his eyes. Suddenly, he could hear the beast, this time moving nearer. The purple light had faded while the flames and the sound of cracking timber had stopped. He could hear the creature snuffling and grunting, not as a wolf but walking upon two heavy legs. The beast roared from the direction of the brook. Trifan stood upright and backed away, his boots crunched heavily in the snow. The lower branches of the trees clawed at him, many were now leafless, their winter fingers pulling at his cloak and scraping his face. He was standing upon the path that had once led him to Tumlinfay's mysterious door, which now seemed an age away; where once deep ferns grew thickly around the track now they were buried under a coffin of snow. Rosewene warmed again at his side. He placed both hands upon the hilt and leaned against a tree. His hearing had sharpened. He was wary but he wasn't scared, some greater power steadied his nerves. Never though had he felt so alive. He looked up. He could hear the breaking of branches and the malevolent heavy grunting away to his left, yet it was too dark to see its form. Maybe, it was Morgalene herself; he had heard so many terrible tales. Suddenly, the beast was upon him. All he could see was a towering two-legged monster, its exposed green skin had a sickly hue, while around its sinewy body, hung the remnants of once rich clothing.

Trifan drew Rosewene from her sheath and the blade sparkled.

The creature, its face still hidden in the shadows, recoiled in surprise, shielding its eyes with long green arms. "Fool!" It rasped. "You cannot escape."

Suddenly, there came a strange sound, of a bowstring humming and an arrow released, followed by a low thud. The creature screamed in agony and staggered back into the thicket of the trees.

Trifan could hear its blood-curdling cries and the grinding of teeth.

His last vision of that demon, the sorcerer Proudsickle, was its hideous red eyes burning out at him from the consuming darkness, to where it had retreated.

From the emptiness around him, a slender hand, warm to touch, clasped his wrist and pulled him from his nightmare. "Come with me." It was the voice of the young lady he had seen before. "Trust in me and follow, come." Trifan felt clumsy as he stumbled over the snow-covered path, following the slender, agile form of this mysterious girl. She uttered not a word as they ran. The only sound was the patter of her bare feet and his heavy breathing. They ran and ran, weaving around branches and the solid forms of ice-covered trunks. They ran for what seemed an eternity until they entered, gasping, into a circular grove of frozen oak trees, illuminated only by the light of a full, yellowing moon. She turned to gaze at him and in that moment as their eyes met his heart was lost. She looked into his green eyes, melted for a fraction of time, then breathed deeply and smiled; she kept her heart in check, knowing that doom was but a kiss away.

"Why are mortals so easily turned?" she thought.

The spell had broken.

Trifan coughed, looked back at her and smiled in return. She was beautiful to behold, even under the dim light of the moon. He had never known a girl in Oakendale to compare. Though they appeared the same age, she had in her eyes and expression a determination and look of someone much, much older. Her face was elfin and her hair was long, so long it swept past her slender waist. But it was her radiant, yet mischievous smile and beautiful eyes, he thought blue, that drew him in again. His smile was now dreamy. Her eyes narrowed and she frowned seemingly now unimpressed with the mortal boy. She brought a hand to her mouth and sneezed.

It seemed to break the spell of seduction again.

"Bless you," he said rather sheepishly.

She looked at him, unsure at what he said. Her smile returned. The boy did possess a quality she liked, her instincts were right. For a mortal, he was handsome and his appearance pleasing to the eye. "So it is you who brings winter to the garden?" she asked while looking apprehensively at the sword by his side.

Trifan looked surprised; her words were musical, beauty for the ear, yet the content harsh. A moonbeam bathed her face and Trifan could see her sharp ears protruding a little from the curtain of extremely long fair hair. Her brow was raised just as Wilfin did when he had scolded him by the clearing at Nim.

"I am sorry I brought the snows," he said quietly, while under the spell of her gaze.

"Well, do you have the key?" she said directly.

Before he could reply, or even begin to understand how she knew, she had reached her arms around him, the soft material of her sleeve touching his cheek and with her long nimble fingers, reached into his breast pocket and pulled free Tumlinfay's strange key.

"But ..." mumbled Trifan.

She placed a finger to his lip and stopped frowning. Then she laughed a laugh that for a flickering moment lit up the dark forest.

"I have been watching the old mortal's house for some time," she said softly. Trifan let her words wash over him.

"We have to leave here now not only from that bearded ghoul but even sommerling feet feel the cold!"

She took the key in her right hand, re-arranged the longbow across her back and then walked over to a familiar squat, lop-sided oak tree. Its branches were creaking and groaning with shock in this sudden winter-realm. The ivy that had once formed a curtain around the broad trunk, now hung in frozen clumps.

"That creature has a name?" she whispered. The sommerling-elf turned to look at him as if searching for an answer.

"I do not know," replied Trifan, his teeth still chattering from the cold and shock. One minute, he was standing in the warmth of Tumlinfay's kitchen and now, he had witnessed Golenwood's destruction, the loss of two new, yet dear friends and the horror of being pursued through the snows by a ghoul.

And yet, being in the company of this enchanting creature seemed to appease all of what happened. "I do have many answers but not that one," he replied with tiredness. "I fear my friends have been killed." Trifan looked down at the snow as tears began to form in his eyes.

She instinctively reached over and touched his cheek.

But as Trifan looked up she withdrew her hand.

"I saw the ghoul's arrival," she said in a whispered breath. "At first, it was a mortal man, tall, with a long beard of snow-white. He wore a dark blue cloak and talked loudly to himself." She looked deeply into Trifan's eyes and was pleased to have found him. She was beginning to feel something for this boy. In her mind, she could hear the words of her father warning her against mortal desire.

Her gaze turned from the boy to the trees behind.

"He does not follow," she said with relief.

"He?" asked Trifan.

"This tall mortal, similar to your friend, the green magician," she replied clearly.

It was strange to hear her musical voice dancing over such grim words. Trifan listened to her talk and though they were in danger his mind wandered and he could feel the heavy strings of love tug at his heart, feelings he had never experienced before.

The sommerling ignored the mortal's sheepish look and carried on talking, hoping it would stir him. "He raised his long arms skyward then smashed two bottles upon the rocks and so conjured up the snow," she continued louder than before. "At the door to the strawhouse he drank from a large green bottle and smashed it against the rocks. He clutched his throat screaming and screaming and in a goblin-voice called, Dragool. Dragool!" she cried, shaking her fist at the sky.

Suddenly, a branch snapped in the deep of the forest behind.

"You called?" rasped a hideous voice from the trees, followed by the loud drip of saliva falling to the snow.

The elf and mortal turned in terror but could see no sign of the monster. "Run!" she cried. "Trifan, we have to reach Noominglade now!" The boy then recognised the tree, the lop-sided oak. It was Tumlinfay's secret door! He cursed his slowness.

"What is Noominglade?" stammered the boy, his feet rooted to the spot.

"It is a door to the Sommerlands," she replied swiftly. "Come, we have to go."

She knew there would be no going back, yet to bring a mortal freely would mean banishment; perhaps even death. It had been a long while since she had set foot back home. She hoped her father had forgiven her.

They had no time to lose, they could hear the branches snapping and cracking behind them and the sound of large limbs moving swiftly in pursuit. Ninfa rushed to the tree, placed her hand upon its worn trunk and spoke in Elvish.

Trifan watched as she placed the key into the diamond-shaped hole, it didn't turn, for a moment he feared he had taken the wrong one, then to his profound relief, saw her push open the large oval door, which ground loudly with the effort. She turned to face him and beckoned him over.

Flurries of snow blew across the cobweb-laced threshold, while before them was a small, uninviting hole.

She seized his wrist and with a strength defying her size, pulled him through the hollowed space.

Trifan looked back for a final time and to his horror,

this creature had bounded into the clearing, its gruesome face in full view. Remnants of a long white beard remained, while a blue cloak hung in rags around its green sinewy shoulders.

It was then that he knew he was looking at a sorcerer, one in particular, Proudsickle; or what remained of him.

Before the creature could strike, the sommerling had dragged Trifan into the dark recess of the damp smelling tree and swiftly locked the door. There they both waited, breathing heavily from tiredness and shock. Trifan could see the light of her eyes sparkling back to him in the gloom. "The power of Noominglade shall protect us," she whispered. "You are safe for the moment."

Trifan did not notice the tear in her eye.

Outside, in the dark wintry forest, the ghoul that was once Proudsickle, squatted, like a beast, unable to control his large teeth that would grind together, then release odious droplets of saliva into the snow. He studied the lop-sided tree and smiled. In a small part of his mind, he had won, he had remained a sorcerer; he was still Proudsickle. He tensed, waiting for Morgalene's reply. Thankfully, it never came. He knew he had found one of the many portals into the realm of sommerling.

Maybe Tumlinfay had already visited? Another secret his old friend had kept from him, maybe he should have killed him at the cottage but the strange masked apparition before him, of his old rival, had simply vanished before his eyes. What was Tumlinfay up to, sporting such a symbol of summer? Still, he had no time to dwell, he always was eccentric.

Proudsickle twisted his face into a smile. He had, at last, found what he had always wanted.

His mind darkened if indeed it could get any darker. He would stride into the realm of sommerlings and seize power. He knew from Grib that there was a king, once powerful but now too trusting, too old; yes his name, what was it, Barcorn. King Barcorn.

He would abandon that old hag Morgalene; control or kill Grib and from there build his own empire. How evil makes the mind grow stronger! Again, he tensed. No reply came. He smiled again if a smile it was. What a fool he had been; the door before him was just an old tree, one he would surely smash his way into.

First, he tried to break the door, yet it remained fast. Then he squeezed his new talons into the door recess, yet it wouldn't move. Then he roared and charged at it but it remained intact.

The tree felt the impact, but it smiled, the ugly fool would never get in. That was why he was chosen for Noominglade, tended to and fed rich soil for the last thousand years.

Dragool sat in the snow and wept then he gnashed his teeth and then roared in fury. They had all escaped once again. He could even smell Rosewene now, her sickly-sweet scent emanating from the tree. He knew they were in there laughing at him. How he wept.

Trifan and the sommerling listened to the noises beyond. Once they had stopped, the faery rose from his side and glided her long fingers around the rim of the tree's belly and in an instant, small lights, some green, others blue, or yellow, began to illuminate the inside of that ancient trunk, which appeared to Trifan, much broader than he had imagined.

She laughed, took off her bow and laid it upon the ground.

"I won't need this." She looked up into his eyes and laughed again. "I have you now to protect me, do I not, Trifan?"

"You know my name?" he asked in amazement.

"Mortal boys are very noisy, my ears are sharp, as you can see," she laughed. "They can hear everything."

Her blue eyes locked into his. Trifan blushed and felt awkward. "Where do we go now?" he asked quietly. "We shall follow the steep road down to my home," she replied softly.

In the far recess, where the lights were less bright, Trifan could see a small round door.

Suddenly, the sommerling murmured a strange verse, over and over. Trifan, still entranced by her beautiful voice, sat and listened. He couldn't understand the words, or what they meant but then, as if by magic, the small door swung open, revealing beyond a smooth tunnel, not lined with tree roots and crumbling earth but illuminated again with many small lights, lights that covered not only the walls and curved ceiling but the many broad steps that descended sharply down into the earth, down into the mystical land of sommerlings.

The faery took his hand and looked into his eyes. "Yes, I am a sommerling, an elf and yes, you are quite fine for a mortal boy." She laughed once again as she swirled around him.

Joy surged in Trifan's heart. "Who are you? I don't know your name and yet you have saved my life."

"Who am I?" she replied teasingly. "I am Ninfa".

16

A Spirit of Summer

TUMLINFAY watched from the garden's edge. He could see the creature, once Proudsickle, scream in fury, its claws scraping at its eyes as if temporarily blinded, then run, in great loping strides, toward the forest.

The magician shook his weary head. What a fool his old friend had been. His own magic had startled this creature but it had left him weakened. Despite Tumlinfay's great age and endless aliases, he had never experienced a surprise such as this.

Proudsickle, who he thought had been tending his great manor at Grendeline, had in fact been meddling in the wastes of Mortenden.

So that had been the reason for his five-year absence. He wondered who else had been persuaded by the Grand Wizard's smooth tongue, to follow him on an expedition south, into the lair of Grizilder.

Yet hadn't he kept secrets from the Order himself? He guessed his good friend Rumbleweed and perhaps Bedevere had travelled to Mortenden, even at their ripe old age and poor health, one with a broken heart and the other with a broken body. He knew they both wouldn't be returning. It was Proudsickle who had raised Morgalene from her grave!

As he witnessed Proudsickle's new horrific form he guessed that it was a gift from his new queen. He felt a grim sadness at Rumbleweed's demise; he always cherished their friendship, ever since their shared dormitory at Garfax.

Tumlinfay's long fingers felt around the rim of the mask. He could feel the power of the mask surge through his veins once again, his own wonderful gift from innumerable centuries ago, even before the time of Gilindon, when the island had been called Britain.

The magician pulled the wooden mask free and turned it over in his hands, looking down at its mournful gaze. He wiped his long sleeve over the carved face of oakleaves, smiled to himself and placed it carefully into his small bag.

The mask was ancient, from the very beginning of time. It was a gift from Mother Nature herself, Bronia, when the world was young and sommerlings were the first to walk the earth.

Beautiful Bronia had watched him grow for many a year, approving of his pure heart and noble manner and in time loved him as a son. The gods had many worries, not just with the alluring blue sphere of the earth but with other distant worlds, yet still they listened to Bronia, of her concerns for the well-being of all life and for a weapon to protect the vast myriad of her creations and so they gave her a magical gift, one imbued with the power of life itself, to give to a spirit she favoured the most to ultimately do her bidding and to keep the cycle of seasons turning.

Tumlinfay smiled, as he remembered how it felt to place the mask upon his face for the first time. He could breathe the scents and smells of all the seasons at once, while his body surged with many feelings, of the joyful jostling of spring buds, to the rich perfume of summer, the bracing gusts of autumn, to the frozen power of winter.

Bronia had chosen her servant, her new prince. His name then had been Nuner, still was but it was a name he now gave to the mask. He felt much more comfortable as plain Mr Tumlinfay.

He had worn the mask in many battles, saved many kings and queens and helped restore lands after famine and pestilence. He had been at Arthur's side as they defeated Mordred, had weaved an enchanted forest, as Herne the Hunter, to help a band of outlaws and had once summoned storms to wreck an invasion. Was he really that old!

But nothing had shocked him as much as tonight. All of Proudsickle's oddities and eccentricities had been unveiled. Tumlinfay rested upon Eldsmoreth for now he was feeling weak. The little surprise for his old adversary had drained him of much-needed power. He knew though that he could have killed him at any time. But he needed Proudsickle alive. He gazed over to his home, now frozen under a blanket of white enchanted snow, another of Morgalene's gifts that for now could not be undone. He breathed deeply, unsure of what to do. He knew Proudsickle had come for the boy and guessed that Trifan had fled into Whitewebbs with the sommerling.

Oh yes, he knew, he had sensed her at the forest's edge. He winced suddenly, as a sensation of lost love spiked his heart. His last love had never returned to him. It was a terrible feeling that would never leave him, an itch he couldn't scratch. He hoped the boy though would be safe, not just in body but in spirit, such a similarity to the boy Arthur, once, four-thousand years ago a great king of Britain. He smiled at that thought, though hoped this boy would be less trouble.

Something deep down knew that this sommerling was sound of heart. She was agile, fleet of foot. He knew Trifan was safe for now, he could feel it in his bones. She would be taking the boy to the hidden kingdom, a final door he had tried for so long to enter, yet the maiden Noomin would not let him in, despite being the spirit of nature. Sommerling spells were too strong. He knew that Trifan had taken the key for the lop-sided tree and that with this elf creature they would both pass the tests of Noomin.

He was a bright lad, Rosewene had chosen well.

Tumlinfay would have to follow Trifan to the Sommerlands in time, but for now he would have to look for his friend Sirifix. In the commotion, they had separated and Tumlinfay feared the worst, for his friend had a secret, once comical but not now. Sirifix had a condition, which he was struck down with at Garfax University, one which caused great embarrassment at the time. At times of great stress his friend would change his form, one that he hadn't chosen. Tumlinfay knew that Sirifix had turned into a fat black cat!

17

Sommerlands Awake!

NINFA and Trifan descended the steep steps for what seemed an eternity. The myriad of colours in the stone calmed the boy's nerves.

The elf's scent was heady and alluring, it was a sensation that made him feel alive as if he was leaving his weary mortal body behind. He wasn't sure if he was in Elbion still, or had reached the Sommerlands.

Ninfa would sometimes cast a glance behind, yet she knew the ghoul could not follow.

As the final steps came to an end, her heart became heavy, for though she was Barcorn's daughter, luring a mortal, a thudler, to the hidden kingdom, was a crime. She thought of her father, though powerful he had aged and was too trusting. She also thought of the other's arrival that spring evening, only ten weeks ago. He was a sprite from the north, he said. That creature's name was Grib, blessed with a silver tongue and fair looks; even if his manner was coarse and his black eyes were tinged with a streak of cruelty. It was said that this Grib had been banished many years before and had once served her father as a scribe. Though he looked different upon his return, taller and with a nose and ears less pointed, her father had greeted the traveller with open arms, almost as a returning son.

All in the kingdom could see this newcomer as nothing more than a sorcerer, laying spells upon the old king's mind. She shuddered as she recalled how Grib gradually took control of the Sommerlands, by whatever spells, introducing his own councillors and guards, or inquisitors, as he liked to call them. Then the vile sprite had turned his attentions to her. How he would follow after her as she walked through the meadows, or lust after her as she bathed in the secret pools and how once his sinewy arms pinned her to a tree, while his long, green tongue slid over her cheek and how he shrieked in anger as she pushed him away, observing how his once fair looks had now faded, his giant ears, now coarse and hairy and his nose extending beyond his ugly pointed chin.

Whatever magic potion he had taken had now disappeared, leaving him true to form, a sommerling from the shadows.

Yet, her father, Barcorn, still trusted Grib, would listen to no objections, almost doted on him. That was when the punishments began and Ninfa decided to leave home, leave her father's side for a while and journey alone to the mortal world beyond as a wanderer.

As the final steps came to an end her heart became

heavy, for though she was Barcorn's daughter, she knew the penalty for luring a mortal to the hidden kingdom. She knew Grib's inquisitors would arrest her upon her return and not just for luring a thudler.

Grib's power would have grown swiftly in her a few weeks away, maybe her father would not save her after all.

She paused and pulled her hand away from the boy.

Was she making the right decision? If left alone, this mortal, this Trifan would surely perish. The world he knew was coming to an end. She was now his only hope. She would look after him, of course.

Ninfa wiped a tear from her cheek. He could never become a sommerling. Love was not an option, for a year together wrapped in love, was nothing, just dust to blow away. For the cold would eventually come for them both and destroy them into the ground. She had to keep her hand from his, not to breathe his scent, or touch his face.

Trifan felt Ninfa pull away and he felt his heartache.

Her eyes now rested upon the small door, the fabled door to Noominglade. Trifan followed her gaze and in the dim light of sparkling stones noticed not a door, but a large haunting face staring solemnly back at him. His mouth dropped open.

"That is the door of Noomin," whispered Ninfa quietly.

Trifan could feel the growing distance between them as her eyes avoided his. He tried to catch her glance but she skilfully avoided his gaze. The moment he looked down though she would quickly glance his way.

Her heart jumped. She could feel a sense of foreboding, as though fate was guiding her towards a doomed love, a broken heart and finally death. She blinked, as the voice of the boy broke the silence and the spell.

"Who is the face in the stone?"

"She was the maiden Noomin," replied Ninfa sadly. "She was a nymph of the Whispering Forest, one of the seven kingdoms of Sommerland."

"What happened to her?" he pressed, guessing that it was a sad tale.

"She became mortal, to follow her love." Ninfa stared coldly at Trifan. She could see how young he looked, how innocent.

Her fingers glided over the brow of Noomin, whereupon the stone door began to glow in a faint light.

Trifan was sure he could see her solemn mouth turn faintly into a smile. Perhaps he was mistaken.

The door moved outward, letting in creeping fingers of sunlight to that once dim space.

Trifan had to shield his eyes. He had left winter behind at Golenwood and now the warmth and light of summer had returned to his world.

Ninfa nimbly pulled herself through the small round door. Trifan followed somewhat clumsily, prompting the elf to laugh aloud. As the boy crawled through the door, he found himself sprawling upon a carpet of sweet-smelling grass, surrounded by small clusters of fragrant cowslips. The door suddenly ground shut, making them both jump.

As Trifan kneeled in the long grass, admiring a greenness that he had rarely seen in Oakendale, Ninfa began to dance around him.

Soon she was laughing and smiling, she then turned swiftly out of view, spinning away like a leaf in the wind.

The magical music of her laughter filled his overjoyed senses and completely banished the memory of the ghoul at Golenwood. He raised himself, brushed down Rosewene, whose hilt now warmed in his palm and took in a deep breath, looking around in awe at this new land.

It had grass, it had trees, yet it was different. High above, a clear blue cloudless sky reflected brilliant summer light upon a neat forest of trees, not a wood, as such, because all the trees were arranged neatly, in ranks, like an orchard.

The trees were tall and thin, with bark the colour of silver and large oval leaves of light green that fanned upward into a rounded shape, finishing to a point at the top. It was, as if, many gardeners had taken their shears to each and every tree, tending them with great love; not a wild place such as Whitewebbs, where the trees were old, gnarled and struggling for light. This forest grew in harmony, each tree seemingly happy with its own space and, as a faint summer breeze rustled their neatly clipped bodies, he was sure he could hear the silver trees whispering amongst themselves and the musical sound of bird song coming from deep within their branches.

Ninfa smiled. "This is the Whispering Forest and the

fairest trees in all the Sommerlands." She came and stood by his side, her scent teasing his senses. "These are the lucky ones," she continued. "They are the silver lindens, the oldest trees in the world. I am sure they are talking about us now, see how the widest tips of their fingers touch their nearest friend, then pull away."

"The trees would never harm us?" stammered Trifan.

She looked at him, tilted her head a little and then laughed, before turning away from his side to dance upon the grass once more.

Not far from the Noominglade, the branches of a silver-linden rustled and a pair of curious brown eyes peered out.

The small figure began to breathe fast and with excitement. Never would he have expected this. Two figures, one obviously a thudler, had entered the hidden kingdom! The figure then let out a loud sneeze, a habit he did whenever he got excited.

A warm breeze fluttered the surrounding leaves, disguising his own clumsiness; just in time it appeared as one of the figures, the female, looked his way. "Fool!" he cursed to himself, why did he always have to be so clumsy.

He was after all a well-respected watcher, promoted to senior level, to stand guard at the door of Noominglade. He was told there were thousands of doors scattered across all of Sommerland's seven kingdoms. Yet this door was important, for the legend of Noomin's doomed love intrigued and terrified all folk. It also made them fear mortals and the power they hold within them.

There were whisperings of evil mortals trying to sneak in and destroy their ancient realm. He watched with growing curiosity as the female, elf he guessed, danced around the gangly youth and began to sing. Hadn't she heard of the rules, the punishments that were now in place; his heart was torn, he hated reporting back. He had his own position to worry about, for behind him, somewhere, others not so friendly were watching him. He sighed heavily and peered through the leaves, his own dark green tunic of oak leaves, contrasting to the mellow green of the linden tree.

He thought he recognised her laugh and her dancing did look familiar. Then he saw the hair, the extremely long fair hair, whose ends she tied under her belt. Was this? Could it be? Yes, it was! The small figure clapped his hands, unashamed at who noticed.

It was Barcorn's daughter, Ninfa, returning at last!

She had famously kicked Grib between the legs and fled from his evil grasp, only last spring, vanishing to the mortal garden beyond. The hideous sprite was the laughingstock of the hidden kingdom since that memorable moment. Shame others haven't been so brave since.

The small watcher groaned aloud, he knew he had to report back to his captain, Sliga.

If he let her through, unchecked, the punishment would be horrendous. It was well known that the inquisitors used a machine upon all traitors, one that would split a sommerling apart as they squealed for mercy. He put his head in his hands and thought long and hard. "I have to warn them," he whispered to himself. It was his time to be brave now and stop being Alcorn the clumsy.

18

Alcorn the Bold

TRIFAN suddenly flinched, as a creature, human in form and no higher than his knee, dropped from the sky to stand directly before him.

The figure in question was a pixie, one who wore an agitated expression, which was at odds with his round pleasant face, a brown face framed with black curling hair and one that was used to laughter and merrymaking. He was dressed entirely in dark green, in shades that shimmered like the sun through a dappled forest in summer.

Ninfa placed a hand to her mouth and suppressed a laugh. She bent down and touched him under his chin. The creature responded by placing a tiny hand upon her finger and glanced up at them both in awe.

"It is you!" he exclaimed, his voice high and cheery, yet tinged with concern. "My dear Princess, I cannot believe I didn't recognise you, I never was much use as a watcher."

Trifan knew he was looking at a small sommerling, so different from Wilfin in appearance and yet they had the same swift movements and darting eyes. This sommerling was dressed in a shimmering tunic and cloak of green that changed shades constantly, while his trousers were brown and had a rough hue of bark. Upon his head was set a rounded green hat, like an acorn, under which his long black curls extended. He was truly a handsome creature with a voice that flowed musically like a woodland stream.

The creature was anxious and his large brown eyes darted from Ninfa, to the boy, to the linden trees that grew in their neat lines all around.

"My bold Alcorn, what troubles you?" whispered Ninfa. The pixie couldn't take his eyes off the boy.

"Trouble has brewed already," he replied, his voice steady but high. "We are in trouble, we have all been found out!"

"Come," said Ninfa, calmly reaching out for the sommerling's hand. "We shall find a secret place to talk."

They were indeed being watched. Two pairs of malevolent eyes were fixed upon Alcorn. One of the hidden creatures spat to the forest floor below in contempt. These were the followers of Grib; a name all sommerlings came to fear, a name that had arrived from the north and now crept stealthily amongst the shadows and dark places of the realm, corrupting the foolish and the lost, while growing from strength to strength.

"My, my, Drax," croaked the thin voice of Smegler, a notoriously foul and evil pixie, who had been banished to the depths of the Darkening Forest. "This will be such a reward. Grib will bestow golden gifts upon our heads, for sure."

Both sommerlings were predictably dressed in grey and their lips daubed with an ink, crow blood mixed with nightshade, a mark of allegiance to their new master.

"Never did trust that half-pixie," muttered Drax, a nasty sommerling who took great pleasure in wing-snapping when called upon. He would dearly love to practise that skill upon Alcorn, whom he hated as a traitor.

"Alcorn was never one of us, always Barcorn's helper that one; well, his old king will soon lose his crown and his head!"

Both the pixies laughed uncontrollably. Some say this new madness sweeping the Sommerlands was the result of mortal-nightshade, not just daubed on sommerling skin, but drunk as wine and added to the water of the many pools and fountains, while slowly, gradually, the plant's noxious poison seeped into their veins, corrupted their minds and destroyed all good sommerling sense.

Drax sat upon a spindly branch of a linden tree and thought back to Grib's arrival in the hidden kingdom, many years after his long banishment. It was amazing how many sommerlings still worshipped the ground he walked on. Of course, he had many oddities. When he had swept in upon the back of a giant raven, dropping before the very feet of a startled Barcorn, his face was different, more pleasant on the eye, his teeth were an unnatural brilliant white and his once lidded eyes were now sparkling like two emeralds. The king had foolishly trusted him then, this wandering sprite with his small box of tricks. These were gifts he said that came from a higher order. Drax spat to the ground. One such gift was the seeds of a plant, whose berries would bestow great power. The plant, known as mortal-nightshade, grew not in the Sommerlands but the rich mortal lands beyond the doors. Soon Grib had begun destroying ancient groves of hawthorn and holly and began planting his gift.

Sommerlings would gather around curiously as the nightshade quickly sprung from the soil, coiling and choking great swathes of the king's garden. The plant's berries were large and enticing, yet surprisingly odourless and tasteless.

Soon, Grib had produced a fine wine better than honey-mead and stronger too. The wine was addictive and was served at all the banquets, only a handful of sommerlings, including Ninfa, refused to drink it. Even then this magical fruit found its way into the streams and wells, there was to be no escape from its wonderful properties.

Drax licked his lips, he could still taste the berry upon his green tongue, sticking to his bristling coarse hairs. He had much work to do before he could raise another glass to his mouth, or re-stock from the winery. First, he had to inform his superiors about Alcorn and the two figures that had slipped from view. He thought he recognised the female, surely it couldn't be? The rumour was that she had left her father's side to marry a mortal and spend a year tending his goats and milking his cows! True love was always so over-rated. He breathed sharply, for his throat was sore once again. Smegler's foul face was looking at him trying to read his thoughts. "You know who that was, my friend?" snorted Smegler. "I think it time to blow the horn, to warn Sliga and Snapper we have guests!"

Grib was sitting on his new throne when word came to him of the intruders. He stopped gnawing upon the bones of a boiled pigeon and spat the sinewy flesh to the ground. His magic had grown with the help of Morgalene and he had subdued this vast kingdom easily, not by sword or arrow but with wine! He was bigger than when he had first entered Grizilder all those months before, he had kept his brilliant white teeth, but his nose had grown again and his chin had become more pronounced. He drained another goblet of fine wine, burped loudly and then cast the cup to the bushes behind him. He pulled up his vast purple coat and a broad smile spread across his ugly face. He had at last found his queen. It helped that his height had improved of course, for he was nearly as tall as an elf.

Ninfa moved with such speed and grace that Trifan felt clumsy as he tried to keep up. When he had climbed down a bank away from the linden trees, he found he had entered a large grove of holly bushes, their leaves the darkest green, while their berries the brightest red.

He could hear the high voice of Alcorn whispering to Ninfa, who was kneeling before the stout sommerling.

Her extremely long hair trailed over her knees and splayed out across the ground covering Alcorn's small brown boots.

Trifan came and sat beside them, sitting cross-legged, as he rested Rosewene upon his lap. By now he was tired and extremely hungry but ignored his stomach and listened keenly to the sommerling.

"We all have to leave now," gasped Alcorn, his high voice cutting through the silence. "You have been missed, my sweet Ninfa, but your father, the kingdom, is in peril. Something, some dark magic has poisoned the land." Ninfa cried out, it was the first time Trifan had seen her vulnerable. Even sommerling emotions were stronger and truer than mortals'. He watched her beautiful face tense and her brow furrow. But when she spoke, she was composed, her clear voice resolved.

"I wish to see him Alcorn, see him at once."

"I am afraid, however much I love you, I cannot take you to him," replied the pixie solemnly. "You see, he is a prisoner, a captive, along with all your supporters."

Ninfa placed her face in her hands and remained still and silent. Alcorn looked over to Trifan and shrugged.

"I'm afraid our world is changing and for the worse," said Alcorn sadly to the boy. "You will be no safer in the Sommerlands. You have to leave here, leave at once." Ninfa rose to her feet. Trifan looked at her in awe. She was the most incredible sight, his heart pounded hard as he studied her tall form, so young, yet she appeared ageless.

Her movements were fluid and confident, of someone older, someone who had seen much life. Maybe she had loved before. He felt too young, too clumsy to win her heart; yet if he did, he would surely die after a year of desire and torment as the magician had told in his sad tale. His heart sank.

He looked up and found himself staring into her eyes, her nose almost touching his own. She could sense his unease and she briefly touched his chin, then she turned from his side, pulling the blue cloth of her tunic around her willowy form.

Ninfa breathed in sharply. How foolish she had been, with her childish wanderings, her singing to the birds and dancing by the many streams in the mortal land beyond. How she had neglected her responsibilities, her friends and her dear father. She stroked her brow and then she cried aloud, "Father!" Her voice was so strong it rustled the holly leaves that seemed to crowd and bend towards her. "I have not been the daughter you wished for. I am sorry." Alcorn looked on, wiping a tear from his eye while his right hand rested on Trifan's tunic.

"Different from your mortal brides, I think."

"I think you are right, Alcorn," replied the boy.

19

The Dark Pool

DEEP in the shadows of the Darkening Forest, Grib sat upon his new throne, a high seat of power where judgements were made and sentences passed. It was carved from yew and decorated with runes, strange symbols and mournful faces, which peered out from behind thick tendrils of black ivy that clung to its sides.

He sighed with pleasure and smiled to himself smugly as he sunk into the deep seat, for his once stunted stature had grown, as had his long nose and chin, ever since he had received those wonderful gifts from Morgalene from within the dark vaults of Grizilder.

Not one for vanity, he looked once more in his round mirror and admired his longer face and whitened teeth. The wine was indeed working, yes, a few more wrinkles and hairs but he was now as tall as mortal man and as strong.

His mind wandered again as he closed his eyes, one pleasure eluded him and it was peace, peace of mind.

Her voice would always enter his head, always stop

him from resting. But for now, all was silent and his mind travelled back to that distant winter's night in Tangleroot Forest, the night he first met that strange mortal. Grib then drifted at last into slumber as he dreamt of the fateful encounter.

At the same time, deep in the forest of Whitewebbs, Proudsickle was dreaming the same dream.

Distant Dreams

In the far south of the shire of Camelon there grew an ancient forest of immense proportions. Some say it was the oldest collection of trees in the realm of Elbion. There was after all strange awe and magic surrounding that brooding group of wrinkled oaks, giant beeches and gnarled yews.

In the freshness and green-cloak of spring and summer, the sinister side of the forest was hidden from view. In fact, to most who strolled around its green borders, it was a soothing and pleasurable experience. Wildlife teamed throughout its rustling alleyways and swaying treetops, particularly birdlife, whose species were too numerous to mention.

But it was now the deep of winter, there were no visitors, no scampering of vole, or mouse and no cheery sound of birdsong. All that could be heard was the malevolent calling of a lone rook and the constant snapping and cracking of frozen branches. But before the trees could awake and the dark woodland spirits begin to creep, there came another sound to pierce the silence, a strange unfamiliar noise for that bleak time of year.

The forest remained still and watched. Now and again a branch would move, or an eye set within a broad trunk, would suddenly open and then shut.

But the newcomer to that secret realm moved on, like most mortals not noticing the mysteries of the winter woods.

"It's a rider," whispered one beech tree to another.

"I haven't seen one for years, many years," whispered his friend.

"Centuries at least, well over a hundred cold ones I'd say," marvelled the first tree.

"Ah...what a sight to relieve the boredom and shivers!" responded the second tree eagerly. "Let's have some fun," urged the first tree. "I'll see if I can swipe his pointed hat off. Ah, there she goes, ha ha."

The rider pulled at the reins, frowned at the offending tree and dismounted to retrieve his hat.

He felt a sudden drop of rainfall upon his face and noticed that the skies were darkening rapidly. He mounted his horse and then began to feel the creeping fingers of cold.

"Come, Spindle," he urged, "We have to make camp soon, it's too far for us to return to Garfax tonight."

The large horse stamped its hooves in disapproval and

shook his shaggy mane nervously. "Come, my friend," whispered the rider soothingly, "We shall be safe enough, trust me." The horse sniffed his master's face and then moved off, reassured by his warm words.

Shortly, the rider came upon a dark, stagnant pool of water set at the base of a small hollow. Even from some distance, the water smelt foul and uninviting, yet something enticed him to stay awhile. He found the moonlit pool and its clearing enchanting.

"Yes," he said, sighing with relief. "I think we shall stay. Look, there is even an outcrop of rock. We shall shelter until the storm passes."

The rider tethered his faithful friend and sank back under the rock, brushing a thick nest of straggling ivy cords. He lit a clay pipe and sat watching the outline of the dark pool and the surrounding skeletal trees.

As the winds became stronger, so the dark, billowing clouds eventually covered the once bright moon.

At first, the rain fell lightly, tapping rhythmically upon the thick bed of dry, fallen leaves; then as the winds began to whip, so the rains fell with ever more power, lashing down with menace and venom. Suddenly, the rider became aware of movement within that grim glade.

He sat impassively and watched. At first, he thought his mind was deceiving him, but no, the branches of the nearest trees appeared to beckon to him. It was then that the rider looked on in horror as that brooding, twisted forest, became very much alive.

Faces contorted upon their hoary trunks, they were gnarled and looked malicious, yet full of glee. Eyes began to open, as did large toothless mouths. Now their branches didn't sway, or beckon, but rattled violently in the cold night air.

At first, the rider pressed deeper under the rock, terror filling his heart; he had never seen such magic before. But something in his mind began to reassure him, to lure him out from his hideaway, yes, so it was, the trees were calling out to him.

"Dance!" they called, "Come to the dance."

The rider climbed to his feet and moved out from the shelter until he stood in the driving wind and rain.

From out of the shadows they came, faeries of the night. The rider looked on aghast as the winged creatures darted and wheeled by the pool's edge. They were not the pretty creatures of popular myth but devilish folk, naked, or with skirts of grass. Under a curtain of rain, they now sprang, laughing and screeching with delight. Most danced with one another, but two, or three noticed the mortal stranger in their midst and flew to his side. They smiled at him, revealing razor-sharp teeth. One faery grasped his hat while another pulled his long black beard.

Now, as the rider was dragged to the pool's edge the foul faery music began. Some beat a drum, others played flutes or whistles. The cacophony of music was fast and furious, sending that ghastly collection of creatures into an even greater frenzy.

"You are beautiful!" cried out the rider, totally bewitched.

"Then baptise you we will," came a harsh voice from the darkest shadows.

The rider turned and came face to face with a large, hunched faery, sneering and extremely ugly. Suddenly, the music stopped and the dancing ceased. The large faery looked the rider up and down and then spat into the mud that now stuck to their feet.

"Please, my bearded friend, do take a drink from the pool and be blessed!" He laughed and then embraced the mortal.

The rider looked around the hollow and saw beauty and cunning in the faces staring back. He smiled at them; for some inexplicable reason, he wanted to stay, to be part of this strange magic. "Yes, I will drink from the pool," he said. "The water looked so beautiful in the moonlight."

"Then bathe your wise head and become one with us!" screeched the faery. "Come, embrace the power of the shadow and forsake the cursed sun."

The faery led the rider by the hand, bade him kneel and then pushed his head under the water. "Do you like the taste, oh bearded one," cackled the faery.

The rider spluttered backwards with a strange smile upon his face. "I do, as fine as wine," he gasped.

The gathered faeries laughed together in a chorus of screeches.

"Then the magic of the pool has blessed you with many powers," replied the large faery, smiling wickedly.

Suddenly, three green creatures, all without wings and human in form, approached the rider. They embraced him and kissed him. The rider melted into their seduction.

"See how my Dryad wives adore you!" The tall faery smiled to himself and rubbed his hairy hands.

As the rider laid down amongst the damp leaves and mosses with one green temptress after another he failed to notice his beloved horse being led away into the deep woods beyond.

The following night the rider was sitting by the pool's edge with the faery. Both were chewing succulent sinews of meat from a bone.

"What brings a mortal such as yourself into the woods at night?" asked the faery curiously. Before the rider could reply the faery spoke again. "Were you sent to spy on our secret ways, or were you easily seduced? The beautiful pool drew you so, I could see it in your eyes."

"There is a beauty, a dark mystery about the water," answered the rider. "Something in the rippling mere that I do not yet understand."

The faery rubbed his pointed chin and looked intently at the stranger. "Do you know that the pool only draws creatures of evil intent? That is why you intrigue me, my mortal. Are you evil? Does malice and darkness lurk behind your black- beard and within your deep eyes?"

"I have never thought of myself as evil," confessed the

rider, lying a little. "Sometimes I think of power, of wealth, even murder but nothing really bad. I always sleep well at night."

The faery then laughed, his mirth hideous to behold. "I think I can trust you now, you have passed the test. Your heart is black, your thoughts impure, you will be good to teach, of that I am sure."

Some smaller faeries, only knee height, tried to listen in on their conversation, but the large faery sent them scurrying for cover. "Begone my children, play once more in the shadow."

The faery leaned nearer to the mortal. "Having someone like you will be of great help to me and beneficial to you."

"Go on," said the mortal. Curiosity was beginning to consume him. "What can I do to help you?"

"I know where great wealth and deep secrets can be found. But I need help, mortal help. Now I can tell by your hairy chin that you dabble in mortal magic, that you have power."

The mortal smiled and nodded. "Yes, yes I do. But I am still learning, still searching for answers myself."

"Is that so?" muttered the faery. "Well, we have a lot to learn from each other. You can show me secrets from your world, show me mortal magic."

"And in return?" asked the rider leaning forward. The breath of the faery repulsed him, but he held his nerve, curiosity was skinning him alive.

"I shall give you a key, a very special one."

The rider pulled back and looked at the faery with a strange glint in his eye. "A key?"

"A key to the many doors that lead beyond, to our very own faery realm." It sniggered as it noticed a change in the mortal's expression.

The rider's mouth dropped open. "But don't you dwell in your secret places, such as dark woods, wild fells and deep caves?" The rider's eyes glinted ever more brightly. Would he be the one, the first mortal to learn such secrets?

The faery chuckled and then began to laugh in that hideous cackle once again. "Live here? This is but a playground, a garden sweet, full of succulent mysteries but it is not our home."

The faery leaned forward, his breath washed over the rider like a foul-smelling breeze. "There are many doors that lead beyond. You will never see them, I guess. You are near one now." The faery smiled gruesomely.

The rider's eyes were bulging with excitement. "Show me, I beg you. You must show me a door!"

"In time," croaked the faery. "But as I have been the first to offer a gift it is now your turn my wise mortal to give me what I want!"

"Yes, of course," he stammered. "I will give you anything, anything, just to gaze beyond the door."

Grib smiled and leaned nearer. "I know you come from the house of turrets, from Garfax; a wise place truth be told. A house of secrets and magic!"

The rider wondered how the faery knew this and pulled back from the creatures. "Yes, I dwell there and yes it has many ancient manuscripts and yes many secrets, many mysteries, but alas, they are locked away, hidden within our deepest vaults." The rider then flashed a smile. "But I do hold the keys, such is within my power."

The faery smiled broadly, showing off his sharp teeth. "Good, that is very good. Then I can see we can do business." He placed a spindly arm around the rider. "Then let the mortal and faery worlds unite. My name is the Grib, by the way, a most powerful prince of the other world." The mortal fingered his tall hat, his heart was pounding with excitement, but a niggling doubt made him wonder what he had got himself into. Then his mind turned and he swiftly thought of the riches of the faery-lands and the marvels to come and where doubt left him, greed and a thirst for knowledge began to consume him.

The Grib sat gazing at the mortal curiously. "You haven't told me your name, oh bearded one."

"My name, of course, how rude of me. I am Proudsickle, keeper of the library at Garfax and holder of the keys."

Faeries hidden behind in the grove jangled their instruments like the sound of rattled keys; and then the foul faery music began again, as once more the rain lashed down.

So this was how all the mischief and trouble began, with a chance meeting by a dark pool, deep within the forest of Tangleroot.

As an old Elbion saying goes, "If you dig too deep in too many dark corners, then one day you will surely uncover evil."

HERE ENDS BOOK ONE